CLARICE

Her journey through life

Harriet Maxwell

authorHOUSE®

AuthorHouse™ UK Ltd.
500 Avebury Boulevard
Central Milton Keynes, MK9 2BE
www.authorhouse.co.uk
Phone: 08001974150

First published by AuthorHouse 7/27/2011

ISBN: 978-1-4567-7750-0 (sc)
ISBN: 978-1-4567-7751-7 (e)

Prologue

'When your Daemon is in charge, do not try to think consciously.

Drift, wait and obey.'

From 'Something of Myself for My friends Known and Unknown' by Kipling

Chapter 1

I don't feel well today...Dreams out-witted me last night. Chaos reigned in my head, just when I thought it was clearing.

Years of talking to various guides, sages, clairvoyants and therapists, wasted!

Today I shall regroup, look out on the forlorn grey winter, too icy to walk out; stare blankly at another day-time television show; try another crossword (not cryptic) just something to straighten my mind, not irritate it; check my emails...again, then stroke the cat.

Tonight, valium?

The kids were so cute, Jamie and Lois.

My Mum had wondered how I would manage with literally no previous experience with children, nor with house-work. Worst of all, I knew nothing about cooking!

But the Elliots who had taken me on were desperate, having had a disastrous series of au pairs, home-helps etc. With both of them working full-time in the City, they had had to get someone in pretty quickly. A "safe pair of hands", they said. Well I would be that!

It was a pity, to my mind, that mums wanted to go to work so much these days, and not look after their own tots. This meant that they only saw the children at weekends, because, by the time they came home in the evening, the kids would be fast asleep in bed. All for the money and status! Why overstretch yourself like that, missing the best years of your kids lives. Why let somebody else watch each step of your babies growing up and miss out on seeing them change into children, with personalities all their own. Miss seeing them learn to walk and laugh and play; miss taking them to nursery, and then on to school... Well, at least Dave and Kathy Elliot told me that they had no intention of sending Jamie and Lois off to boarding school at seven.

How could any parent do that anyway? What was the point of having kids?

The first supper I made for them was ever so slightly burned and they told me I had set the table wrong. Apparently, I had put the knives and forks on the wrong sides, and the spoons shouldn't be at the top. It puzzled me that they bothered so much about this sort of thing, when they had willingly entrusted their kids to me, an untrained nanny; a girl previously quite unknown to them. It's not like they knew my family or anything about me. We lived miles away, in Cheshire.

My name was Clarice and I was sixteen. I left school with no GCSEs, just hope in my heart and a 'pleasing manner', or so I'd heard people say; plus I knew that some of the boys at school said I was pretty. I thought I could make it up as I went along. Life, I mean. As time went by I discovered that this usually works quite well.

I was dying to 'see' life, and now my dream was going to come true. I was working near the big city. Living in the country had always cramped my style, this was the break I had been on the look-out for.

It all started when I noticed an advert in 'Lady' magazine.

Back home in Cheshire, where I lived with my Mum and Dad, I sometimes ran errands for my Nan, who was pretty much housebound. This particular day I only went down to the library to take my Nan's books back for her, but flipping through the magazines while waiting at the counter, I saw it, 'couple wish to employ working English girl to care for their two children...etc, etc near Epping forest, on the outskirts of London'

That was it! That could mean my big break! I ripped the advert out, when the librarian turned her back and rushed back home to show my Mum...and, as they say, the rest is history.

My routine was pretty set. I used to get the children up at 8am, always waiting until their parents had gone off to work, usually on black coffee and nothing else. What a way to face the day, on an empty stomach! Both carrying their brief cases and laptops, they joined the rest of the commuting crowd, striding down to the tube, not even chatting to each other. I suppose both their minds were set on their very important day ahead!

In contrast, my day started with a hearty breakfast. Lots of jammy toast and all the kids leftovers!

Jamie was nearly three, and managed to get himself dressed, more or less, while I sorted Lois out and put her in the high chair for breakfast. After their milk and cereal, baby porridge for Lois and wheat biscuits soaked in milk for Jamie, plus tiny bits of cut up toast, oozing with butter, which he loved, I got them ready to go out: But not before I'd hovered up all their remnants. 'Waste not want not' as my mum would say.

Jamie trotted excitedly into nursery. I left him playing with the other tots, while I went off to do the day's shopping. Lois used to doze off almost immediately as I pushed her round the little shops, lulled by the motion of the push chair. There were still no supermarkets in this little town, so I could choose fresh produce each day. First, meat for supper, at the butchers. He always made a crude remark, and stood in the doorway of his shop, in his bloodied apron with a slight smirk on his face.

Never mind, the green grocer's pavement display was lovely. Rosy apples, green beans, exotica from far away and potatoes and sprouts, which I bought.

Finally, big treat of the day, the bakers! Strawberry cookie or cream éclair, custard tart or chocolate doughnut? What a choice! As I gazed, I tasted each one in my mind. The big decision made, I pushed Lois home to tuck into the cake of the day. Lois slept throughout my delicious dilemma.

After a week or two of settling in, I realised that on my low pay I wouldn't be dashing up to London on the tube, like my employers. Apart from the high fares, where would I go, who would I go with?

On my free weekends, I used to travel back to see Mum and Dad, so the only possible time I could have reached my Mecca (with other things being equal) was when Kathy and Dave came home early enough for me to go out, in the evening.

Occasionally, on a weekday Kathy, returned early enough for her to see the kids before their bedtime, and then she worked on her laptop, late into the night; but I still wouldn't have had the time or money for a trip up to town.

I checked the time of the last tube, and the cost and knew that, as things were, I didn't have the time or the money.

Epping Forest is, strictly speaking, on the outskirts of London, but, it was still much too far away for me.

'Plan B', I would look nearer for my fun.

Six weeks after starting my job, I saw a notice in the corner shop about the local youth club. Good! It wasn't affiliated to a church, as that might cramp my style, again. The notice said the club was held at the scout hall on a Friday evening, from 7pm onwards. I made up my mind that somehow I would get there.

So when Kathy was a bit more relaxed than usual, I asked her if it would be possible for me to go out and make a few local friends. I told her about the Youth club.

She smiled sweetly and said that though, in theory, she heartily approved of the idea, it was going to be difficult for her to get back form the City in time for me to go. She sympathised about how cut off I must feel, with only meeting the other kids' mums at the nursery and not making any friends of my own age, but it was still an emphatic 'No'. Her job entailed late planning meetings every Friday, and that was unlikely to ever change. I felt very cross. I hated my plans being blocked. I tried hard not to mind, thinking something else would turn up; And then quite unexpectedly it did change, and sooner than expected.

Kathy arrived home from work one day, with a glow on her slim face.

"Clarice, Great news" she said "I've been promoted to another department. I will be home a bit later most days, but I they've given me a half day on Fridays. You'll be able to go to your club, after all!" That was only a month after my original request, so 'YIPPEE' I'd soon be club-bound!

I described Kathy as having a 'slim' face. That sounds rather a strange description for a face. In fact it was angular with a pointy chin. Attractive, in a kind of executive way. It was the first time I'd ever really noticed her looks, though I'd thought she always looked smart and efficient; someone people would take notice of; Someone who would always look confident. Look **right**, in fact, for every occasion.

I decided, almost unconsciously, to style myself on her.

However there was one big obstacle to this. I was curvy with a round face and big toothy smile. At home my friends had always teased me about being buxom and needing a brace, but actually my family all looked a lot like me, and were cuddly. 'It's in the genes' they said, but a lot of it was down to my Mum's delicious cooking; besides boys seemed to prefer me round and cuddly, so I didn't care. Or rather I hadn't cared till now.

The girls at school used to call me names, because of my chubby appearance, but I never cried. I just shrugged it off.

My Mum said that girls were just jealous of me because I was so smiley and got more wolf whistles than them.

I think that's why Kathy and Dave liked me, first off, thinking I looked comfy and maternal, and would be good with the kids…and that was true. Jamie and Lois and I got along just fine.

No, that's not quite true, about my family I mean.

My sister Prue was so picky with food, and picky with everything in fact, so she never stood a chance in hell of getting fat (or even comely as my Dad liked to call it). She was his favourite, always getting little perks and the best titbits of crispy fat off the meat. He used to pick the marrow out of the roast lamb bone with a skewer, for her to suck up. You couldn't do that now anyway, because of BSE.

Little Trevor was eight years younger than me. I always thought he was a kind of after-thought, a bit puny and not quite the full picnic. Worst thing of all was his fingers, or rather lack of them…three missing off the left hand, with only the stubs to show where his fingers should have been.

I looked out for him in a sisterly way, but I could never quite look properly at his fingers. I think my Dad was scared by them too. He'd wanted a big strapping footballer type son, but instead he begot a weed. This made him angry, and I used to try to protect Trevor, especially after our Dad had had a few. It was weird really, I felt both protective of Trevor, but repulsed by him at the same time.

And my Dad, though he packed a punch, was thin; wiry thin, from hard graft.

So when I said my family were all plump like me, I really meant my Mother. Big, fat and huggable. Wonderful cook, but always tired from trying to persuade Prue to eat, Trevor to buck-up and be 'normal', and Dad to be soothed and oiled, so he didn't 'start'. I was my Mum's little helper, not all that little, either! We were more like sisters, than mother and daughter.

Kathy was a far cry from the 'mother' stereotype, who had raised me.

The first Friday I went to the club, I was shy. Everyone seemed to know each other, they had 'in' jokes etc and I was wall-flowered. Still, I liked the juke-box music and the general hubbub. And I must admit I eyed up a boy who was standing by the counter. He grinned a bit and turned away, but as we were leaving, he strolled along side me. "Hiya! You new here? It's Mike. See you next week?" Before I'd answered, he disappeared into the gloom, and I went home to consider.

"Kathy" I said, on the following Monday when she got home from work "Can I have a word?" We had a real girly chat about boys and clothes and things, but the most important of the 'things' was contraception. "Clarice, you must see the GP and get on 'the pill' " she said
"But Kathy I don't even have a boy friend, I've only been to the club once and no-one knows me there yet. There's **no** chance of me getting pregnant!" I replied, but later after thinking about it, I realised she didn't want to lose a good nanny to the pudding club.
As I was green, I still believed men romanced you, like in 'Mills and Boon', after courting you they asked you to become engaged to them, and then, with your full consent, 'made love' to you. The truth, of course, was quite different. The youths at the club only went there for one thing, otherwise they'd be down the pub drinking (mainly under-age) or else watching football with their mates.
On the third Friday, Mike had me behind the Scout hall. It was quick, it hurt and I thanked my lucky stars he used a condom.
Two days later, I started on 'Minuet', a pretty sounding name for a chemical that would temporarily halt my fertility. Kathy took me down to the GP's surgery herself.

It was after this, that I began in earnest to emulate my employer.

I watched her at supper, refusing seconds. I watched her in the morning with her black coffee. I still stuffed myself with food because, as I told myself, I needed the energy to keep up with the little ones. Or so I conned myself. The kids were indeed lively and full of fun and definitely hard work, so this was a reasonable justification. But it seemed the less Kathy ate, the more I stuffed. I began to really take pleasure in cooking the evening meal, and I started to study new recipes, while Jamie watched TV and Lois, dear little thing, gurgled to her toy lamb, in the playpen.

Every night I made a different dish, and tried to improve the way the food was displayed. Dave relished it and often had seconds.

"We've found a treasure in you Clarice", he would say, "It's like coming home to a restaurant with your cooking. You must give Kathy the recipes, so she can cook like this for us at the weekends, when our friends come round. It's absolutely divine."

But Kathy protested. "Oh Clarice, this is gorgeous my dear, but it's not doing my diet any good!"

I didn't know she was on a diet, she was pencil thin! Why was she dieting?

I was thoroughly enjoying myself now. They liked me. I cared for the kids well. I could spend any amount on food, and then cook it up into elegant dishes. I could always polish of the leftovers, and at the end of my working week, bonk Mike behind the Scout hut, after Friday's club night. What more could a girl wish for?

Though my cuisine improved by leaps and bounds, the bonking didn't. It didn't hurt anymore, but I never came!

And so life continued, till one family Sunday back home, while helping myself to seconds of pudding, my Mum said

"Clarice, do you think you ought to dear?"

"What do you mean, Mum, it's my favourite, Queen of puddings."

"I know dear" she hummed and haa-ad "but you are putting on a bit of weight."

"Well I'm not as fat as you!" I shouted, burst into tears, and flung out of the room.

All the way home I reflected.

I thought again of my childhood home, how different it was from Kathy's household, with hers consisting of two perfect parents with two perfect children.

First of all there was my sister Prue, sweet looking, petite, and picky! It annoyed Dad, despite the fact he always favoured her with tasty morsels! It made me sick!

Then there was Mum and I. We had always tried our best and hardest to help Trevor. Poor stunted little kid! But the worst thing about him, the thing that crept into my dreams and changed them to night mares, were those three missing fingers! I'd never looked really closely, but I knew he had stumpy vestiges where the fingers should have been. The ends sucked in and twisted like tiny ends of sausages when the stuffing's run out. Hideous! I'd always made sure I'd held his other hand

So, Dad drank. I remember the times when we all went to bed early, even Mum, and on a good morning after, he could be found, snoring on the couch downstairs and we would tiptoe round, till he came to. Then life would carry on as normal.

But I also remember how sometimes after a 'heavy' night, we shuddered under the blankets, fingers in ears, to dull out the noise of him stamping around downstairs, shouting for Mum. Then next day she'd be sporting a bruise or two. Once, we saw she had a black eye. But no one remarked on it.

How did I escape from all this? I simply ate.

Not that I was fat! I was comely? With quite a pretty, somewhat toothy smile.

I had never consciously felt any resentment at being Mum's unrecognised help and support, but any feelings that could have bubbled up, were soon hushed by seconds of 'treacle pudding', another of my mother's delicious specialities.

And now, Mum had even kicked that crutch away from me!

After a few months at the Elliots, I began to look more closely at the couple.

Dave was a pleasant enough, run-of-the-mill sort of guy. Posh. Was he middle or upper class? I wasn't sure. He did seem to love his kids, but definitely didn't want to spend much time with them. Obviously, not in the week, because of work, but weekends? Golf seemed to obsess him. I'd overheard Kathy on the phone to a her friend Jan.

"Yes, we'd love to come over on Saturday. Can't manage Sunday. Sorry. Dave's golfing. No, next weekend he's away too" Apparently, he was trying to reduce his handicap at golf, and was hoping to be elected Club captain the following year.

Not much spare time for the children then!

My thoughts turned to Mum, struggling to keep the home happy. Dad working hard, sleeping in front of the TV, or down the pub, on pay day. Were all men the same in different ways? That sounds odd, but you know what I mean, always finding something to do that was more absorbing than being at home with the family. Would I ever find a man who was more of a story-book dad?

Then there was sex. Were there lovers who charmed and considered you? Kissed and stroked their way into your affections. Loved you for what you were and brought you to resounding climaxes? Or was that just a fantasy world. The only orgasm I'd ever had, so far, was self-administered. But then Mike probably had to do it quickly, before we were caught? I'd had fond dreams of his technique improving, but if anything, he came quicker than ever, and recently, I had even noticed him eyeing-up other girls at the club.

How was sex between Kathy and Dave? Obviously they had it, as they'd produced two kids...but there was no sign of much romance between them now. Did they indulge in a lengthy fore-play, ending up with her astride? She was quite forceful. Or was it just a quick in and out between linen sheets, rather than behind a scout hut?

Same process, different location!

Oh well! I didn't dwell on this too long as so far, I much preferred food to sex.

And I was beginning to feel I'd had enough of Mike, and while I was happy in my job, I was beginning to feel there must be more to life. Yes, there must be more, full stop! 'I'll set my sights on Kathy.' I thought, 'I'll model myself on her, but first I need to find out more about her, she was so very self-contained I thought it would be like pulling teeth.

The breakthrough came from Kathy herself. Becoming less and less tired by her new job, which though better paid and having more kudos, was less exacting, (so she told me later) she became more approachable, with time to chat. And, she was getting fed up with becoming a 'golf widow'.

I became her confidante, and she became my mentor. We started having long chats about my future too.

"Clarice, even though I love having you here with us, and the children adore you, you are a clever girl. Have you ever thought of bettering yourself? You could start evening classes and maybe get some GCSE's" I was chuffed, but couldn't quite see this happening.

First, I must become more like my mentor. And so the modelling began.

Kathy was slim as a crisp. I guess she'd be about 8stone. Fancy that after having two babies. My Mum had said that's why she was fat.

"You never lose it after giving birth, Clarice" she'd said "Your figure goes, especially after having three!" her words rang in my ears. I made up my mind never to have babies, if that's what it did to you. My Mum regularly asked me if I thought she looked as 'big as Mrs So& So' over the road. I always cheered her up by saying "No, Mum, you're not as big as her!" But I had never really understood why my mum didn't do something about it, because I would have tried to lose weight if I hated my appearance as much as she did. Yes, I would definitely have done something about it. I **will** do something about it, before it's too late!

There was no way that I could stop stuffing the delicious food I made, but I could get rid of it other ways. Laxatives? They were the answer.

I bought some Ex-lax from the chemist on the way home from a shopping trip, and started on them that evening.

1-2 tablets, it said on the pack, but I thought I'd try three, as I had to make a start quite quickly. First, I went to the bath room and behind the locked door, weighed myself. 13stone! OMG it was worst than I thought. No wonder I'd had to resort to wearing those stretchy, velvet trousers from the bottom of my case. Had they been my mum's outgrown ones? I shuddered!

Watch Kathy. That was the key.

Next morning I woke with agonising stomach ache!

I used to have a similar pain every month, but since starting 'the pill' it had almost disappeared. Next thing, I rushed to the loo and the doors opened. Diarrhoea flooded out. Afterwards, I felt considerably cleansed. But the pain returned, in fits and starts, all through the morning, with diminishing results. Perhaps only two pills tonight.

Weight loss was slow with laxatives. I couldn't eat less. I lived to eat. Eating was my passion! I thought again, and then remembered the Ancient Romans, from my school history books. They used to tickle the backs of their throats with a feather, to bring up one lot of food to make room for the next course. Vomiting! That was the way forward, the only quick way. But how did I do it? I wasn't sure. So I waited till after one extra rich supper, that Kathy and Dave had raved about, and cleared up in the kitchen as usual. Then, before stacking the basins and pots in the dishwasher, I cleaned out each one of them with my finger, licking all the creamy sauces. Now I did genuinely start to feel a bit sick. I'd try tonight.

So, after I said goodnight to Kathy and Dave, and peeked in to check that my charges were safely in the land of Nod, I locked myself in the bathroom and knelt in front of the toilet pan. Desperately I tried to throw up, just as I had as a small child, trying to regurgitate the enormous supper I'd so recently enjoyed.

But it wouldn't work, however much I retched. I concentrated hard, and retched some more, still nothing! So then, having no feather, I put my finger as far, down my throat as I could reach, and gagged. Up came bitter bile. It didn't work this time however hard I tried, and I started to feel faint, and terribly ashamed. I promised myself that no-one must ever, ever know what I was trying to do. It would always be my secret.

I slunk to my room and wept, waking every hour with the taste of acid, like paint-stripper in my mouth.

The next morning I awoke with a sore throat and coated teeth. My plan hadn't worked...yet. But I **would** do it! I'd practice and practice until it did work. Then I would end up looking like Kathy, and no-one would ever know how it came about.

My relationship with Kathy become more fluid, as fluid that is, as any relationship between a young, un-educated, plump country-bumpkin and an older, sophisticated and articulate business woman could ever become!

But the friendship was definitely helped by my gradual and increasingly obvious weight-loss.

The technique, that I had now perfected, and that must always remain nameless, was working a treat, and now I could eat as much as I liked without any worries.

Kathy was amazed.

"Clarice," she said "you're looking slimmer and slimmer these days, and you certainly don't starve yourself. You must tell me you're secret. I have to try and exist on black coffee, to even stay the weight I am! How do you do it?"

'No' I thought 'it is my secret, and no-one is **ever** going to discover it!'

"It's just the kids, Kathy, they run me ragged, while you probably don't burn much energy, sitting at the computer most of the day" I lied.

Even Mike noticed I was slimmer "less to grab hold of C!" he leered, 'Well.' I thought, You won't be grabbing hold of me for much longer."

Kathy had said I should start to think of getting some GCSEs.

"You go round to the high school, where they have the evening classes and bring me back the prospectus for the Autumn term. We can go through it together. If we find some good courses for you, maybe I could get home a bit earlier a couple of nights a week and, if you leave the supper ready, I could see to the children, and you could start the classes."

She told me that she had pulled off a few deals at work, and the bosses were really pleased with her. They considered her a 'Rising star' in the company, and were happy to give her some lee way over the time she needed to spend with her small children.

So two years after I started at the Elliots, I enrolled for night school to begin the maths and English GCSE courses. Maths was on Fridays, so that put paid to rolls in the proverbial hay with Mike.

When I walked into the classroom, on that first night, I weighed 10stone 5lbs, wore size 14 jeans and a smile on my face!

Next term, my aim was size 12.

As months and terms flashed by, Jamie and Lois grew bigger and I grew thinner, copying Kathy in lots of ways purposely, but also becoming more like her by diffusion. Just being in her presence affected how I was becoming, on the outside, at least. I'd cut off my shoulder length curls and now had a slick bob. I still wore slimmer fitting jeans, having given those baggy old velvet trews to OXFAM, and I started wearing shaped shirts which showed off my boobs to advantage. They were still large, but almost pert, above my shrinking waistline.

When I Looked in the mirror, I still looked fat, but the scales didn't lie and they declared me to be only a pound or two over 9stone! I had added biology and drama to my GSCE subjects now, and with the added stress, found myself sitting up late studying into the night to get good results. Did I do this for me? No, I did it for Kathy, though she didn't know it. I wanted to **be** her, with a 'nice' husband, good job and a lovely home.

More often than not, when I sat up late with the books, a sudden emptiness would come over me. A longing, an overwhelming sense of hopelessness, a yawning inner abyss, which had to be filled. I slammed the books shut and tiptoed downstairs in the dark, to the fridge. I eat whatever there was. Leftover chicken pieces from the children's tea, the rest of the apple and blackberry tart doused in double cream, some sweet caramel puddings, meant for tomorrow's supper. Then opened the freezer, there would always be organic chocolate ice cream to dig into. Only half a tub left! Well I could easily finish it off and buy a replacement tomorrow. And so it went on. Whatever took my fancy I polished off until I sat back on the kitchen floor feeling glutted, feeling disgusted, feeling utterly hopeless... 'I'd never come to anything,' I thought 'I'll never be like Kathy.'

Then I crept back upstairs to the bathroom, and knelt at the toilet to make my atonement! Cleared of sin, I returned to bed and dreamed of a future in which Kathy and I were intermixed. I was almost her! I was slim, in control and successful.

I enjoyed the new studies at the college, and made a friend called Jo. She worked as a junior in a local paint firm in Woodford. Only a gofer really, but it paid quite good money. She was fun to be with. Sometimes at weekends we went window shopping in Ilford, or we met up for coffee at the local breakfast bar. Once we went to skate at Queensway ice rink in London. It was brilliant, though I collected masses of bruises. This was my first trip on the tube.

Since I'd stopped going home every weekend, I started having more fun, but I did feel guilty about Mum. I wondered how she was coping with Trevor. Was he ten or eleven now? He'd be going to be start at secondary school next year. But, hey-ho, Jo was showing me more of the life. I needed, to break out, to even start to be as successful as my idol. I was eighteen now and it was definitely time to spread my wings.

Jo too was at a crossroads in her life. She was sick of living at home, with her parents, and keen to move out, but couldn't quite afford it unless she got a better job. She applied for an interview to become a librarian. They liked her immediately, she always came over as so friendly and competent, plus she had a few GCSEs with good grades. She was given a job at the library, in Woodford. We talked of sharing a flatlette near to her job, but first, I also needed a job, with better pay and at least some prospects.

I passed all the exams, and with Kathy's help applied for a job, working as an assistant in a chemist shop. There was an empty flat to rent, above the shop. I wasn't sure how to give Kathy my notice, thinking she might be upset,but once again she came to my rescue. She said that as her kids were getting older now, Lois was at nursery full-time and James was at big school, she thought that with help from her network of friends, she could sort out the kids pick-ups. It also appeared that Dave's job kept him out late at business meetings, therefore my delicious suppers weren't so necessary!

Kathy said that she could rustle up suppers or get ready-meals delivered from the supermarket, which had recently sprung up in the adjacent town. In the beginning there had been local anger and petitions against it, but in actual fact it proved a boon to most working mothers, because it stayed open so late.

"I'm not pushing you out, Clarice," she said "Of course, you can stay as long as you like, but you do have great potential, and now with your good results, you need to move on up". I could have hugged Kathy. My role-model had come up trumps again, only wanting the best for me. It didn't occur to me then, that all might not be going well in her life and marriage. Her 'fantastic' life that I was aiming for, might, after all, have become as potentially crumbly as mine. Whatever was going on in her life, she insisted that I better myself, Saying "Clarice **your** life is on the up"…and up. I was too young and inexperienced to understand her undertones. That maybe her life, or money flow, or even her marriage was in trouble. I didn't know the saying then that 'All God's children got troubles', and, even if I had known, I was much too young and selfish to care.

Chapter 2

The Chemist's manager interviewed me and took me on. Jo and I moved into the flat above the shop, and life improved over night. Everything was shaping up better than I could have expected, and more quickly. 'Amazing,' I thought later on, 'how things in life can work out so well.'

Life in the flat, with Jo was also taking shape. She had always lived with her parents, where, I gathered her mum had waited on her hand and foot. My Mum had never had the time to care for me that much, so even before I started to work as a home-help, I'd known how budgets, food shopping and cleaning worked. At first, I did everything at the flat, until a bit of resentment kicked in. Jo was quick to pick up on this, and she drew up a rota for jobs. Despite the rota, I preferred cooking and somehow she was the better cleaner, so we gradually fell into a pattern. She left a bit earlier in the mornings though, to get to the library, down the road, while I only had to go downstairs. It worked perfectly.

There wasn't that much money coming in, so nights on the town were still out. It was then that Jo asked if I'd like to go with her to **her** youth club, which was held in St Winifred's church. This was what was known as a 'low' Anglican church. She'd been going for a while, but had never mentioned it to me, while I was working at the Elliot's; but then I'd been tied up, balancing work with studying, so we had mostly only done things together, like Saturday shopping & hanging out at the local coffee shop and never discussed other parts of our lives.

Yes, it would be something new. Meeting a crowd of 'Holy Joes', How suitable going with a Jo, who I had never particularly thought of as holy. At my school everyone had sneered and joked about Christians, so I'm afraid it had rubbed off on me. The jokey t-shirt with 'Jesus is coming' on the front and 'Hide' on the back, had us in fits of sacrilegious giggles. Club-night was on a Friday, so the next week over we went, to St Winifred's Hall where the youth club was held, and I didn't even demur. At least it was a night out and I'd meet some other young people. A very different sort of youth club this, from the one I'd known. A youth club with a message, which wasn't drink and drugs and rock'n roll, not to mention free sex, if you got 'lucky', I thought this might be just what I needed. Too much liberality could lead to 'goings on' behind sheds, and I'd had my fill of that! Somehow I wanted more now, but I couldn't decide what that more was.

Now I'd left Kathy's house and to some extent her thrall, I still desired to be like her. I didn't want to end up like my Mum, pandering to everyone else.
Nor did I want to stay on, working as a nanny forever, that had just been a stepping stone.
And I certainly didn't want to be shagged by any more yobs.
I wanted change; CHANGE in a big way ...meanwhile I decided I would keep taking the Minuet...just in case!

I hadn't known Jo well enough before we moved into the flat together, to find out how much of her life was interwoven with the Church, and how much the church meant to her.
It was **her** secret really.

I realised then that we both had secrets, the difference being, that now she was more than happy to share hers with me.

During the tea breaks, when we'd met at evening classes, we had chatted about clothes, going shopping, pop music and ,of course, boys. It had surprised me then, that Jo was a virgin, "Saving myself for Mr Right" she'd said.

I thought afterwards that it was pretty unusual for a modern girl of my age, to have never been with a man, but then the thought flew out of my head, and I forgot all about it.

Although we'd laughed a lot and shared many a girly chat, we never discussed anything serious, and certainly religion was never mentioned. Maybe she had been afraid that I would sneer at her, so she was waiting for the right moment. Now, with our new domestic arrangement, the time had arrived.

There was a very friendly atmosphere at the youth club, a lot of milling around, and everyone introducing themselves to me, as the new-comer. They were a bit of a mixed bag, with a wide age range, I reckoned about 14 to 28! Some people were playing ping-pong in the corner and I noticed a pool table and a darts board, towards the back of the room. I found out later that if any new guys came to the club, they were given special attention, to make them feel at home. This was seen to be a form of 'witnessing' by believers, so that Jesus was given a chance.

Witnessing was a 'Must-do' for Evangelicals. It was a chance to save the unbelievers and bring them into the fold. I soon realised that Jo must have been living a huge dilemma over whether to tell or not to tell me, that she was a Christian. On the one hand, I might have laughed and stopped being her friend, on the other, she was worried that she wasn't doing her duty as a born-again Christian, by not letting me know what her faith meant to her; Perhaps she thought she should even have tried to convert me. She must have weighed it up, and maybe discussed it with some other Church members and come to the conclusion that by introducing me to the Club, her Christian status would become obvious. Then I could make of it what I liked. After the chit-chat, the guitar group in the corner struck up, and the free sarnies and cakes were passed round...mugs of tea or coffee, nothing stronger, were handed out to wash the food down, and then the singing started. Sankey's hymn sheets were handed out and a group of singers came to the front and sang some sacred songs. We all joined in the choruses. It reminded me of the Sally Army street meetings, in our home town on Saturdays, but no-one passed round the collection box here.

Finally, there was a short talk, from St Winnies's Curate, quite a handsome young man in a dog-collar, and this was followed by a prayer and blessing.

Afterwards, we all tumbled out of the door laughing and joking together, lads and girls together with no snide remarks, eyeing or come-ons. One lad, called John offered to walk us home, but as the church was only just across the road from our flat Jo thanked him, but said there was no need.

"Well how did you enjoy that, Clarice?" Jo asked when we got in.

"They were a very friendly crowd" I said guardedly, "and I liked the free food! What a great idea. Who pays for it?"

"There's a fund for it. D'you fancy a cuppa"

"Yes please, I'm gasping after all that singing." I knew we both felt too awkward to discuss the evening further, so after the tea, we each disappeared into our rooms, saying it had been a tiring week.

I lay awake that night running every aspect of the evening through my mind. Rethinking all I knew of Jo.

Wondering how this new aspect to my life would pan out. It hadn't been bad but it had been quite embarrassing. I liked the friendliness, the lack of cliquey-ness, the absence of flirting. The free food was a plus, but I couldn't work out quantity, or for that matter, quality control on it. I was a bit embarrassed by the mini-sermon on good works, and by the hearty way everyone said 'Amen'. But I loved the singing, especially those choruses that I recognised from hearing the Salvationists, as a child.

The club atmosphere was such a change from the business world Kathy always carried with her. Her world that I wanted to espouse. But certainly the club's churchy atmosphere was a great improvement on the one with which Dad filled our family home. Christians seemed benign, but oh so unfamiliar!

Would I go to the club again? "Yes"

Would I see Jo in a different light? "Yes"

Would this affect my life? "Not sure"

That night I dreamed of food.

Now that I knew her secret, Jo went off to church regularly on a Sunday, but I only attended the club nights. Once, she managed to persuade me to go with her to the evening service, and I was surprised at how 'Happy Clappy' it was, considering it was affiliated to the Anglicans. I was attracted by the singing and the general sense of happiness that emanated from the regulars, but their hype seemed almost put on. It was as if the congregation were on some sort of legal speed. When I talked to Jo about it afterwards, she said that when some Christians get together, they go a bit over the top. A sort of religious ecstasy, but it didn't get her that way, she said that she just liked the assurance her belief gave her and enjoyed the friendly atmosphere of the church. .

"Would you like to come to one Sunday evening mission service, Clarice?" she asked I'd been waiting for this and said I'd think about it.

Apparently Jo had been converted at an evangelistic rally led by one of Billy Graham's followers. Her parents had been High Church, so she was kind of comfortable in a churchy setting, but wanted something a bit more lively.

A few weeks later, when we were chatting with some girls at the club, John, who turned out to be the Vicar's son, was going round chatting to each group in turn. When he came over to us, he asked us if we fancied a weekend away in Frinton-on-sea. Well, who wouldn't! It was spring, the blossom was out, and this sounded just wonderful to me. I'd never been to the seaside and certainly neither Jo nor I could afford even the idea of a summer holiday.

"Yes" we said simultaneously, we would like to go. Definitely! How much would it cost etc. He said that he would give out the details in the notices at the end of club night.

When John stood at the front to announce the details, my heart sank! I should have known this wasn't going to be a 'jolly'! A weekend of paddling, drifting down the pier, penny slot machines, giggles and a bit of fun-flirting. In my mind, I'd already packed my shorts and tops. And of course I'd thought of the food! Chips with vinegar, in paper cones, candy floss, waffles with maple syrup and cream… I may not have actually **been** to the seaside, but boy, did I know the menu?!

The announcement was of a Revival weekend.

An American evangelist was coming to England to hold sessions in various towns, nationwide. Our weekend in Frinton was to be his first mission weekend in this country, and the idea was to bring souls to Christ. I kissed my chips goodbye.

In one disappointing moment, Spring frivolity was changed into sermons and preaching 'in the Spirit'!

Jo spent a few evenings trying to persuade me to go. After all it was subsidised by the church. I tried to explain to her that it just wasn't the way I'd have chosen to spend my hard earned cash.

Things swirled round my mind. Pros and cons. They were a nice crowd… but a bit weird. Where else had I to go? And who with? I was a bit short of mates. My personality didn't seem to attract that many people. I wasn't a team player.

More, a morose git. I began to hate myself. That night, I looked in the mirror and saw the rolls round my hips and my big bust. ? Too big. Much too big I shuddered, then, when Jo had gone to bed, I went to the kitchenette and I rummaged through the food cupboard, eating one packet of crisps after another. Then I started on the cereal, half a packet, then the rest. There were a few jammy dodgers left, a bit stale, but they went down as well...It was all done very quietly, so Jo wouldn't hear.

Soon, the inevitable! Off to my altar, to cleanse my soul of sins. I quickly emptied my stomach contents into the loo...

And, as I sobbed into my pillow, I realised I hadn't had to do that since leaving Kathy's.

Chapter 3

Two weeks before the Frinton weekend I decided that I would go, after all. 'Nothing ventured...' another of my Mum's sayings! I was rather apprehensive, but I felt I should try anything on offer, to broaden my outlook.

It would be a break from routine, and you never know, something good might come out of it. I paid up my dues. £42 including the coach fares, not too bad, Jo said it was heavily subsidised.

In the meantime, it had been discussed quite a lot at club nights. John told us there would be regular preaching sessions morning and evening, to get the message to as many folk as possible, and bring them to Christ. (I cringed) but in between we would be able to play table tennis, go for walks, chat and meet other young people from all over Essex. The food we were told was delicious, as they would be hiring the same chef as they'd had before. (So, this was a regular event: I logged)

Jo was over the moon that I'd agreed to go. She told me again that she'd been converted at a similar evangelistic rally, when a member of Billy Graham's team had been over from America. It would have to be very persuasive preaching to convert me! But I knew this was what Jo was hoping for and then we'd have more in common.

Butterflies started to flap their tiny wings in my stomach. Their wings grew and they flapped more wildly, until 10 days before we were due to travel, I started to feel very ill. I developed the most horrendous diarrhoea, and vomiting but, in view of my secret, the latter was not the problem. After a few days of watery drinks and various medicines Jo bought up from the Chemist, downstairs, the diarrhoea stopped dead, but it left me with a mouth full of dried leaves. I went on drinking water and sipping orange juice, but nothing improved it and I absolutely could not face food, in any form. I gagged at the very sight of it. I began to panic. Would it stop before our weekend away? That was the big question? I couldn't go away feeling like this.

I decided to 'phone my Mum.

"Mum" I said "I feel really ill and I'm supposed to be going off to some sort of conference at the weekend. What shall I do?"

She was sympathetic, but no help at all.

"It's probably just a virus making you feel a bit raw inside. It's sure to clear up quite soon. Lots of people get it. There's nothing you can do but just wait for it to get better."

'Thanks a lot, Mum!' I thought, but I was really worried. Would these awful feelings really pass, and how quickly? What would happen if I still had them when we got to Frinton. What would I do, if I couldn't eat there?

My panic rose, supposing it didn't get better. I would have to sit with complete strangers and pretend to eat, in public, while knowing I couldn't swallow even the tiniest mouth full of food. How embarrassing is that? Where would I look, how could I pretend to eat? I couldn't even leave any food on my plate, -hidden by my knife and fork. 'What about the third world people who were starving?' All the do-gooders would be thinking!

My stomach felt so raw and achey, but, at the same time, strangely full. The dry, acidic taste was so vile, that it stopped me putting anything into my mouth accept sips of water; even brushing my teeth made me gag.

Two days before we were due to travel, I phoned my mother again, hoping for some more helpful advice this time. "Look Clarice," she said, sounding much less sympathetic than before "I haven't got time for all this. You know how busy I am with the family. Trevor's having a really hard time at school, and your Dad's been put on a three-day week. He's spending the rest of his time at the pub. Pull yourself together and you'll be fine. After all, I've never known you not being able to eat before!"

I hung up.

Climbing into the coach with Jo, I felt very ill. The day of departure, was a Friday, so that meant she didn't have to lose any time off work, but I would have to work two Saturdays in a row, to make up time, when I got back… If I got back! I sat next to her, knowing nothing but that I was rigid with fear and desperation. I couldn't meet anyone's friendly gaze. It was horrible. Although Jo obviously knew I'd been ill, and helped me as best she could, she didn't know how terrible I felt. 'Agonised by social terror' neatly describes it. I didn't want her to know either, I was ashamed of how I felt.

I remember nothing about the journey, though in the dim distance, I'd heard muffled choruses being sung in the coach, by all the other happy travellers!

After our arrival at the Conference centre, everything became a blur, I suppose I was weak from lack of food.

We changed for supper, and I followed Jo into the dining room like a zombie. Someone guided us to our designated table and I sat down, by my name tag. Then as quickly as I could stood up again, grasping the back of the chair, as I realised everyone else was standing to say 'Grace'

Kevin, Hazel, Di and Fran were our table mates. I tried to smile as they introduced themselves, though my lips were stuck to my teeth. Kevin poured water for each of us and as I tried to swallow some down it was as if I was gulping acid saliva and bile in successive mouthfuls. Jo realised I was 'shy', so she talked for me. I was so anxious, but I had no inbuilt capacity to calm myself down. No one had ever taught me to take slow deep breaths and try to relax my muscles, I was panic stricken! Valium might have helped, but at that stage I didn't even know it existed. I just wished the ground would swallow me up! When the food came round, I took the tiniest of helpings, a first for me! Jo looked askance, but did not comment.

The conversation started up, and I was surrounded by bright smiling faces. Kevin told a joke or two and then everyone started to laugh. I suppose they were all a bit nervous too. A strange place; new people.

I took a small forkful of cottage pie, put it into my mouth and swallowed it down, with the help of a gulp of water. I wasn't really sure I could do this, but it did go down. Little by little, I followed it with more tiny mouthfuls, simply because it would have been shamefully embarrassing not to surrounded by all these young people.

Amazingly, as the meal progressed, I began to stop thinking about myself and my problem, and started to listen in to the conversation. Pudding was sorbet, and that slipped down easily and soothed my still my fevered gullet.

At the meeting after supper the audience filled the hall. Again there was a spread of ages from about fourteen to thirty, I would guess, and they were all singing loudly, praises to the 'Lord of all mankind'. Sankey's tunes 'rang my bell' and I started to join in with the choruses that I recognised, albeit a bit huskily! I made myself concentrate on the singing. After that, I focussed on the speaker, who at any other time would have seemed unbearably boring . However my intention was to listen to him, and put my eating problem out of my mind. I decided that this had to be the way to make me forget my difficulty with eating. This, and taking very small helpings, at mealtimes. Eat small bits at a time and focus on whatever else was going on, that was the answer. It was one of the hardest things I have ever done.

After the next morning session, there was a longish break till lunch, and we all went over to the Games Hall. No one else was playing table tennis, so we took over the table and started running round the table, hitting continuously so everyone could join in at the same time. It was a real laugh. When we stopped for breath we let Fran and Di play singles, while we got our breath back. While Jo and I leant against the window ledge to recover our breath, two College boys moseyied over to our table and introduced themselves to us. Di and Fran continued their match, while the boys chatted with us. Rod, the taller of the two, had eyes only for Jo.

Not eyes like Mike, lascivious and undressing, just laughing eyes conveying sincerity. Or was it just a clever trick?

I got Aidan's attention. He was the one with the thick lips and melting brown eyes. Well, I've made him sound more attractive than he was. Little did I realise that this chance encounter over ping-pong, would eventually change my life. Nor did I realise then, as I was still green as French beans, that a candid Christian countenance could hide an irrepressibly, rising cock!

This weekend Christian conference had a hidden sub text. It was a venue for match-making!

But from then on, I could eat again.

Why do I always talk so much about food?

Because food and I were locked in an interminable battle. Each of us taking it in turns to gain the upper hand.

Food has always ruled my life.

Comforted me, when my mother had no time.

Soothed me, when my father roared.

It's surfeit sickened me when I was stuffed.

Food then got one up on me, and made me unacceptably fat.

I retrieved myself esteem by regurgitating the excess, finding

I could eat any amount and still stay thin. So I won that round! Had I conquered food?

No, I had won the battle, but not the war.

There was that little, inner voice, that I always disregarded, saying

"There is more to your secret, Clarice than you realise, and one day you may find the key". 'Piffle!' (as my Nan would say)

But for now, thanks to the House Party, Sankey's choruses, and, of course, Aidan, I was in remission!

At the grand final Evangelical meeting, I walked to the front and gave my life to Christ.

Everyone was expecting me to, and why not! Why wouldn't I fall in with their deepest wish for me? They had all been so kind, praying over me and offering me undying comradeship.

I had a lot to be thankful for. I could eat again. I had met Aidan. It didn't seem to matter to me that I hadn't been blinded by a great light on the road to Damascus, nor did I fall to the ground that night in a hypnotic trance.

The counsellors said not everyone did.

I was saved, "Hallelujah, praise the Lord!

Miracle of miracles, my appetite was back,

I was OK. Amen.

Being 'courted by Aidan was strange. But good in parts like 'the Curate's egg'

How applicable, because he came from a very Christian family, and his two older brothers were already working as Curates in parishes up North. His Father was an 'Oversight' in the Plymouth Brethren meeting; (lower down the church hierarchy, than Free Church), and at home he ruled the roost totally, with a rod of Christian fervour.

He had a bristly moustache and beard, and was very dour, hardly speaking at meal-times apart, from saying Grace at the beginning and end of each meal. I found him quite scary.

Aidan's mother, was much more jolly and belonged to the low Anglican Church. After I had be designated as Aidan's 'girl friend', she always asked me over to afternoon tea, on Sundays, with delicious homemade chocolate cake, her speciality.

Aidan and I walked and talked together, holding hands, for many months.

He told me that he was keeping himself pure for the woman he would meet and marry. The New Testament taught celibacy till marriage and then faithfulness afterwards.

I was impressed by the ideals, but what about me, how did I feel? I didn't tell him I was already on 'the pill', nor did I tell him about my dealings behind the Scout Hut. It seemed an awful long time ago now, almost happening in another life. I reckoned if I did tell him, he would forgive me ,because that had been before I was converted, but would he still want to be with me knowing I wasn't a virgin and what if his mother found out? I decided to say nothing.

She had delivered a homily to me one Sunday about the lusts of young men and how provocative girls could lead them astray.

"Clarice," she asked, "have you any idea of the force of men's sex drive?" I had but I wasn't going to tell her what I knew. Aidan and I had moved on to 'heavy petting' a welcome change from his marshmallow-lips type of kissing. His lips were so prominent that they didn't leaving much room for his tongue to protrude, but I felt his cock, hard and huge through his cavalry twills. His mother must have seen a change in how he eyed me over Sunday's chocolate cake, because the next thing I knew, she arranged for him to study in Greece for seven weeks. That filled up his entire long College vacation. The time we had planned to have fun together. But he always did what mummy said!

During that long, hot summer my life became tedious again. Work, church, the Club. The postman delivered frequent post cards from Aidan, with pictures of classical Greek statues and ancient buildings on the front and the backs covered by tiny, spidery writing assuring me of his undying love…Pre mobile phones, this contact was all we had. I hung on to my new but wavering faith, with lots of prayers to keep the food armies behind enemy lines, and bring Aidan back to me. I generally felt more 'normal' but slightly sad. Probably because I was missing Aidan and his mother's chocolate cake! At the end of the summer and more or less straight after Aidan's return, he went up to live in College rooms for his second year. I thought 'Yippee' away from his mum and church and the influences of his family, he would weaken and we would finally get it together.

We made a date for me to go up to visit him for a weekend. He met me off the train and after greeting me with a perfunctory kiss, we walked hand-in-hand to a local café, frequented by students, for tea. He told me students were not allowed to have girls in their room after eleven, so he had booked a separate room for me to stay overnight. He told me that he would walk me there later on after we'd chatted, and then pick me up again on Sunday morning, after breakfast, and we could go to morning service at the College Chapel. "Matins is beautiful there, Clarice" he said "They have the most wonderful choir. You'll love it." He squeezed my hand.

'Hmmm, not quite what I had in mind' I thought.

At last, we went back to his room for the evening, and then, unsurprisingly, we started kissing and cuddling. As the petting began and quickly became more and more intense and intimate, I could realised his sex drive was overcoming his religious indoctrination! I could feel he was throbbing with desire and I was wet through, so I slipped down to the floor, as if to kneel at his feet in a seductive but not too obvious sort of way. He was on top of me in a flash and within a second of making contact with my still fully clothed body, he'd emptied his load into his trousers.

I was aghast. The prince of self control had cum **on** me.

He sat up and wept. I was terribly embarrassed. I didn't know what to do, let alone say.

He said now we would **have** to get married, whatever happened.

I couldn't wait to get back to the flat.

Jo was out, so I went straight to the freezer and got out the carton of chocolate ice cream that I'd bought the previous week.

I felt the numbing cold ice soothe my gullet, the pain of the too cold chocolate numbing any of my other swirling feelings. I felt too ill to think. I couldn't unravel the confusing thoughts tumbling though my mind. Tonight, food was my drug.

After scraping out the chocolate carton, I started on the pink and vanilla ice which wasn't my favourite but lay sympathetically on the freezer shelf. Then I moved on to the cupboard, 2 packs of Jaffa cakes went down a treat and some old jam tarts, left open to the air. So what! Double cream, Jo's personal treat would cover the stale taste.

That done, I went to the bathroom. Only the second time I had paid my respects (I won't say prayed any more, now I was a Christian) to the toilet since I had moved Into the flat.

In the morning my pillow was still sodden with tears, so the excuse of 'flu' hid my red puffy eyes. Thank goodness it was Sunday. No church today, just some serious thinking.

Over the next few days and weeks I cogitated

What exactly did Aidan mean by saying that **now** he would have to marry me.

After all, coming on me in that embarrassing way, was little more than a wank.

Perhaps he hadn't ever wanked ! Surely that was impossible, or did he regard it as a sin. Had he been able to put sex out of his mind in bed at night while thinking of beautiful, Jesus things, to such a degree that his only relief was through wet dreams, the natural outlet? Had his mother done such a good job of brain-washing him?

If Aidan did want to marry me, when would it be? Several years hence after a long engagement? Were we supposed to remain celibate during this time?

I had heard some Christians stayed 'pure' till marriage, the American 'silver ring thing'

Did I want to wait for sex? Up till now we had been only dreamy and lovey-dovey, but this event had changed everything! He had once said that he loved me, but was this love? Did I love him? Was I **in** love with him?

I didn't really know what the 'in love' feeling was like. What was the definition of being in love?

I chucked the Minuet packet into the bin. Whatever was going to happen now was going to need a lot of thought and discussion. (Could either of us face that sort of discussion, I don't think so!)

Did I want to marry him at all?

The pros were as follows:- He would get a good steady job with his qualifications and buy a nice house.

He was kind. Not the sort of bloke to go down the pub night after night, like my Dad. I couldn't get my head round listing the cons, but I thought, if I could they might outweigh the pros.

He would expect me to stay at home and look after the kids (I suppose he would want children? Possibly a lot??) This I may or may not like.

He would also expect me to go to Church twice on Sunday, and that entailed allowing him to become totally involved in Church organisation and good works. I would be left at home to cope. Would he be so much different from my Dad. Just exchanging the Church for the Pub! Same behaviour, just a different venue. Then I remembered Kathy's Dave, a slave to golf!

I knew and was grateful that Christianity had changed my life in many ways, all for the good, but despite what all the zealots thought, it had not changed my underlying personality. Jesus's 'Sunbeams' had had only shone light on my hopes and fears for the future, not changed them radically.

I was still the same Clarice on the inside, though clad in more modest clothes, and wearing less make-up.

Could I keep up with a guy who offered me that sort of life, while his mind was largely fixed on the after-life?

He would be faithful, assuredly, but his embarrassing performance at the weekend, had definitely made me question my own feelings toward him.

The marshmallow lips had never been a turn on, and now I also had to overcome that vision of him weeping with self loathing over something I had indirectly caused him to do.

I couldn't begin to think what loving sex, in the context of a marriage, or out of marriage, would be like with him, after what had happened, could I?

My flesh started to crawl and I didn't know how I would ever face him again.

And I couldn't tell Jo all about it, though I would have loved to have off-loaded it onto someone. Definitely not Jo, though. She was in a safe and fairly child-like relationship with Rod. They had obviously decided to 'wait'.

I consoled myself over the next few evenings by watching endless rubbishy television programmes, even ones dedicated to dissecting such flawed family lives, that only DNA tests could decide who was in the right. I knew I appeared depressed and I think Jo was afraid to ask what was going on. But she didn't dare, as I had never really opened up to her before. We shared a flat and looked out for each other, but apart from that, our relationship had always been somewhat shallow.

On Tuesday, in the lunch hour, I decided to have my hair cut short, really short. This was going against Christian guidelines, as it said, somewhere in the Bible, that hair was woman's glory and should be kept long. Control was becoming apparent to me... Was this how life would evolve if I stayed with Aidan

While waiting for my appointment at the hairdressers, I flicked through some of their magazines, and in the back of one, I saw ads for Clairvoyants. Should I try to visit one and find out what my future held?

This was another thing totally prohibited by the Church. And, if I went, it would become yet another secret hidden from Jo! It seemed we shared the rent to our flat, but little else.

I searched through all the columns of various weird and wonderful people, healers, hypnotists, chiropractors and osteopaths and clairvoyants. There were eight fortune tellers listed. As I skimmed through the list of 'mystic Megs' one name jumped out at me. Odessa!

She lived near Snaresbrook, only two stops along on the tube, and according to the advertisement, right near to the tube station itself. I took her number down and rang from the nearest public telephone. Jo and her church mates would be horrified if they discovered what I was going to do. They had faith in the Living God and asked for Guidance from Him, and Him only. My mind almost buckled under the weight of so many things to keep quiet about! Was I really a Christian, I wondered? Another conundrum for my sleepless hours! If Jo learned what I was really like inside, she wouldn't want to know me at all, let alone share a flat with me.

She was so pure, walking out with Rod; courting, in the old fashioned way, and always home by 11pm. That's what I had longed for in the past, too, when I was escaping from the taint of Mike. I admired her and wished I too could be satisfied by her simple uncluttered life.

I rang and the phone was answered by a woman with a slightly foreign accent, that I couldn't place. She said she would see me very soon. I wondered if Odessa was short of clients, or just keen to help me.

I had already made up my mind to leave no tracks, so I gave her the false name of Jayne Penduggan. It came to me out of nowhere whilst I was on the tube. Maybe from a novel, read years ago?? And for the same desire of anonymity, I decided to pay with cash, which I had taken out of the ATM machine earlier.

I was ushered upstairs into a silken abode. Obviously, I have never been into the boudoir of a 'lady of the night', but Odessa's room looked exactly how I would have expected such a boudoir to appear. Thick embossed velvet curtains, hung at each picture window, the carpet was pink and deep pile and the chairs covered in deep raspberry, Regency striped satin.

Odessa must be doing better than I had assumed.

She told me briefly, that her main occupation was that of an opera singer, but that as she had the gift of foresight, and was also providing financial support to her Italian lover presently singing for a season at the Milan Opera House, she had decided to continue to giving readings.

The price was £40=00.

Odessa looked impressive, with a mountain of thick black curls, done in something of a pompadour style. She wore a crimson and white, low cut dress, revealing a substantial décolletage. In fact, she, herself, was entirely substantial and rather awe inspiring.

She was seated, and pointed for me to sit on the opposite chair. She took my hands in hers and turned them over and back "My dear you have very soft hands, no rings? I had been careful to remove everything that might have given her any indication of who I was, or what I was coming about, before hand

She then looked straight into my eyes, then, strangely, the gaze travelled through my eyes, as hers became glazed.

"My dear, you have come a long way from your beginnings." Well, I suppose that was true, from country girl, though mother's help, to assistant in a Chemist shop.

"You have recently been through a complete and utter turnaround" I suppose she meant my conversion?

I tried not to nod, but instead of looking straight at her, I dropped my eyes, to give her no hint of whether she was right or wrong. Would she take this change in me, as a form of assent?

"I can see your mind is confused. You have a young man, Yes?" I nodded automatically.

"You have been shocked by his behaviour, He is somewhat strange…his behaviour is unexpected. Yes?" I tried not to move perceptibly.

"You will not marry him" she coughed "there is someone else in the shadows. I can't quite see…. It's hard to define him. He moves in and out of the distance, in a strange way. I think he is unusual… extremely unusual."

"Will I marry him Odessa?" her face changed, she went deeper into herself,

"Will I have children by him?" her face had closed down and she started to tremble slightly "Odessa, Odessa answer me" I said almost shouting, to try and penetrate her increasing oblivion. She started to shake, then, quite dramatically she appeared to call out to someone, somebody far, far away perhaps in a parallel universe. I wondered if she was having a fit, though I'd never seen one in real life. But help! This is real life. What should I do? She wasn't registering my presence at all, and was screaming out in an unrecognisable language, Her face had become quite ashen! As I'd entered her boudoir, I'd noticed a jug of water with two glasses on a tray, on the table by the door. I had presumed at the time that she had been going to offer me one, if her predictions during the session had made my mouth go dry. I grabbed the jug and flung its contents over her. It hardly dampened her lacquered coiffure, but quite a lot went down her décolletage!

I waited till she came down from this heightened state of trance and placed the forty quid in notes on the table, between us. Thanking her, I hastily ran for the exit.

I felt shaken up and wished after all I had asked Jo to go with me. No, that would have been quite inappropriate, because she was almost certainly have thought that Odessa was devil-possessed.

Next door was a café. I hadn't wanted to stop off partly because of the cost partly because I desperately needed to get back to my refuge, the flat. But after the Clairvoyant's outburst, I needed to recover myself, I bought a mug of coffee and sat in a corner slowly sipping it, trying to pull myself together... my mum would have been quite proud of me.

I stayed awhile, calming down, trying not to think of the preceeding half hour.

As I went towards the door, feeling more or less restored, there was Odessa, sitting at a table, looking perfectly normal and calmly digging into an enormous knickerbocker glory!

"Bye dear" she said as I walked out!

Chapter 4

Working at the Chemist helped to fill my days, in the following week. I concentrated on the customers and tried to interest myself in the products we were selling. I watched the pharmacist at work making up all the patients prescriptions and wondered if one day, I might be able to train as pharmacy assistant. It looked quite interesting and probably entailed taking a few more exams. But that didn't bother me, I'd enjoyed studying for my GCSEs, and I found it really satisfying to go into an exam, knowing you had done the revision and could answer most of the questions. I just forced myself to stop dwelling on Aidan, and shut him out of my mind. After a long day at work, I was always so tired. Nowadays, all I wanted to do was to eat, watch a bit of mindless TV and go to bed, shutting the whole world out for the next eight hours. One night as I starting to doze off, Odessa's words came back to me, forcefully. "You have been shocked by his behaviour, he is somewhat strange… you will not marry him!" I knew then, she was talking about Aidan. That half-dream convinced me that Aidan was not husband material, at least, not for me.

Boyfriends come and go, but this one had gone, as far as I was concerned, but, I hadn't told him yet. He wrote to me from College about his studies and cricket, but studiously avoided referring to what had happened between us. I wrote a couple of post cards back, but otherwise didn't bother to contact him. Deep down I felt sure he was hurting and that I should reassure him, but I couldn't, so I simply erased any thought of him from my mind. A coward's way out.

The best thing was, that since my conversion, which I suppose still held, I had felt calmer and had begun to be less controlled by food. I was able to fill my time with work, and the club, and I also joined the church's singing group. We had practices during the week and then sung at the Sunday evening youth service which was held once a month. It was much more fun taking part than sitting in the pews for the whole service. Often the congregation clapped in time to the music or joined in the chorus, adding to the general high spirits. I could see why Jo felt so at home in St Winifreds.

I visited my family more often too, no change there; Dad usually snoring it off in the armchair and poor old Mum rushing round doing everything. But they always gave me a warm welcome and seemed to take more notice of me and like me better now I was just a visitor.

With Aidan out of sight at College, and obviously unsure of how I felt about him, I started to put him and the whole unfortunate business out of my mind. As far as I was concerned, he was past history.

I met Terry through the shop. I noticed him one day working through our stand of sunglasses, trying them all on in turn. He was thin and shortish, but with very sexy hips! He seemed quite suave but I also thought he looked quite old. Well, I was only twenty one and still thought most people older than me were getting on. He was actually thirty two, divorced, but starting to bounce back from post divorce doldrums and beginning to feel at a loose end. (so he told me later) I tried to smile so that he noticed me. The next time, I definitely noticed **him.** I watched him dawdling outside our shop and then, with determination, grind his cigarette out with his heel, and come into the shop, as if something had made up his mind. He picked up some shaving gel and came straight up to the counter, "You've got a lovely smile!" He said to me "D'you fancy coming out for a drink with me after work?"

The drink turned into two, and after three, I promised to meet him again for a meal at the local Italian cafe... Pizzeria really, but Italian sounds more romantic.

Next evening we met as arranged. The service was so slow at the pizza place, that by the time we had finished eating, it was 10pm and I really needed to go home. I had to be up early and downstairs in the shop ready for opening time. But after 3 glasses of red wine, plus I was a bit unsteady and had to hang onto Terry's arm, I didn't need much persuasion to go back to his studio flat for coffee.

Need I say, his love-making was unreal . He kissed and stroked his way up and down my body till I was trembling, and finally brought me to a crashing climax, mostly facilitated by those swivelling hips of his. Sex just oozed out of him. It was a truly amazing to find a man who not only loved sex, but who was also intent on making his partner enjoy it the way **he** did. He fearlessly delved deep into my receptive, soft pink, innermost, welcoming caverns and exploded exultantly, with the words, every girl most wants to hear "ohhhhhh, I love you, Clarice!"

He dropped me back in his van, stopping just short of the flat, away from what would doubtless have been Jo's disbelieving eyes. I crept in, but next morning found she'd gone to bed early the night before with a migraine, so I needn't have worried.

It was on the following Sunday, that I remembered the pill. Was it too late to start now or should I try and get the morning after pill from the GP? It was years before these things would be available over the counter. Sure you could buy condoms, but nothing to swallow. Horses and stable doors came to mind.

I'd chance it and start a new packet of 'Minuet' right away, that should be OK. We'd only done it the once,but what a once! If any act of intercourse had been more designed to fulfil its natural consequence, this had been the one.

From then on, Terry and I were an item.

He worked as a chippy for a building firm, so had really early starts in the morning, usually around 5am. This meant he was quite happy for me not to stay the night, in case I should try to lure him back to our warm bed in the morning and make him late for work. We had pretty regular dates, but only twice a week, as he said he wasn't anywhere near ready for commitment. This made life much easier for me as I didn't have to keep making up excuses to Jo. As it was, Jo was now spending most evenings round at Rod's family home, playing board games or watching TV, so I didn't mention Terry to her. I still went to the church club on Saturdays and met up there with Jo and Rod, because Terry liked to have a drink with his mates. It also meant I could keep up with the singing group, so nothing appeared to have changed much, to outsiders. But inside I was deliriously happy. Terry was my man of the moment. I thought I might be falling in love with him, but it was such a new feeling, that I wasn't sure.

I still hadn't decided what to do about Aidan, but in the end the problem solved itself, as a friend of a friend had seen me with Terry and told Aidan that I was seeing someone else.

He wrote to say he was very angry and heartbroken, in that order, particularly, as by his own rules, he would now never be able to marry.

Were the Christian rules on sex correct? Had God written the Bible containing the rules, or was it written by man? The Bible couldn't be totally obeyed as it disagreed with itself in many places, so to obey it all, one would have to split in two. Did I want to be part of such a legalistic belief system? And yet did I want to part with the hope and state of calm it had given me? These questions and many more plagued me while waiting to sleep, whenever I was alone, and sex free.

Somehow, in Terry's arms the questions dissolved, and sex put me to sleep like a drug.

The sex continued to be good, always fulfilling and comfortably satisfying: But never quite as exciting as those first few times. Or perhaps it was just me. Terry was enthralled with my body and its delights! Always repeating how much he loved me whenever we climaxed.

Five or six weeks went by before I realised that I hadn't come on.

I put it down to all the messing about with 'the pill' when I first started seeing Terry.

Even an overwhelming craving for chips, did not signify, after all that was just the way I was with food. Now the sex thing was becoming slightly less important, naturally my desire for food would start to resurface.

Another missed period and increasing nausea, only relieved by more food, finally gave the game away... to my absolute horror!

I heard Kathy's warning about the importance ringing in my head, too late.

But I had only done it once without 'the pill' cover. Surely you couldn't get pregnant the first time?

So many girls must have thought the same thing. It wasn't my first time, but the first without a condom, or of being knowingly safe on the pill.

I must be pregnant! It was like a slap in the face. Maybe that's why I wasn't so interested in sex in the last couple of weeks. Of course, Nature's whole point of sex was the reproduction of further life forms. What an idiot I had been, completely carried away in the moment, and a little drunk.

Maybe the Christians had a good point, at least their babies would be born in wedlock and no-one would point the finger.

The GP said that as I was keeping the baby I must book in for a scan, and he would arrange an appointment with the midwife.

Why a scan? Could there be something wrong with the baby. Was it because I'd carried on taking the pill while I was already pregnant? I thought of little Trevor's missing fingers, and wondered if that sort of thing could be hereditary. Was this my punishment from God?

How would I deal with it? Maybe it wouldn't be a finger maybe a whole hand, or even a limb could be missing.

With my mind in free fall, I hardly slept that night.

Deformity has always filled me with revulsion. I know its wrong, but I can't get over it. I definitely wouldn't be able to look after an abnormal child. Years ago they smothered abnormal infants, didn't they? Or parents dumped them in orphanages, still did in some countries. It was all too horrible to think about.

I must have slept, fitfully, but I awoke to scalding tears running down my cheeks. I just couldn't do this. If the GP thought something was wrong, I would have a termination and not tell anyone about it, and just live with the guilt.

The midwife's opening gambit at my first appointment was to congratulate me on getting pregnant! Then, in rapid succession she asked me if I had a regular partner, informed me as to how the antenatal period would be conducted, and told me that later we would discuss a birth plan. Then asked me to hop on the couch while she examined my still flat stomach and listened for the foetal heart with the Doeppler. Finally she took some blood to check for anaemia etc. I smiled though out the consultation, as only I could when I was nervous, and I answered all her questions clearly. No one was going to know what was going on in my head. Strangely, she didn't ask about family illnesses or problems.

As I was about to leave, she seemed to have an after thought. "Clarice, I nearly forgot about the dating scan. Dr Jefferies will fix that up for you and you'll get the appointment in the post. It will be at Whipps Cross."

Relief, off an unbelievable scale, flooded through me. Of course, a dating scan ! All my periods were messed up with stopping and starting the pill and they could not tell how far on I was without a dating scan.

Terry said we must get married ASAP. I think marriage was the last thing he wanted at this time, still getting over his divorce and the settlement, but he had no kids from his earlier marriage, so why not? He liked kids, "Pity about the timing, but these things happen, Clarice, my pet." He was so sweet. I wouldn't tell my parents about the wedding, as I didn't want my Dad getting drunk and showing me up.

We married at the registry office, and spent the honeymoon weekend in a small hotel on the front at Southend-on-sea, but we neither of us saw the tide come in or go out!

On return, I moved into Terry's one bedroom flat, forcing Jo to look for another flat-mate urgently. I said I would continue to pay my share of the rent till she was set up. It seemed only fair. One thing I knew, abiding by Church rules, her new co-tenant would not be Rod!

Scans throughout the pregnancy showed a normal healthy boy. We asked not to know the gender, but they told us anyway. By the 20 week scan, we had named him 'Tommy', as his kicking feet reminded Terry of Tommy Steele's dancing, in 'Half of Sixpence' ; The show was a bit before my time, But the name stuck.

Pregnancy was uneventful and I continued working at the Chemist's till three weeks before the EDD. An epidural eased the birth, and Tommy arrived on a crisp December morning much to Terry's excitement. We both fell in love with the baby, and were as happy as any couple could be living in such a poky flat, surviving on one small income, and with all nights broken by the teething and fevers of a young child.

The love we had had for each other was now focussed on the babe and he flourished. We still got on Ok and Terry turned out to be a good Dad, coming home for bath time, changing nappies and getting up in the night to make the bottles.

On Sunday morning, I always let him go to the Pub with his mates, while I went to the Church to catch up with mine. I put the baby in their crèche, and began to sing again.

None of my old friends from the Club commented on the unexpected arrival, nor about me, with my shiny, new wedding ring. There probably had been some gossip, but now, they were probably just glad that I'd been able to do the decent thing.

Jo said she'd missed me, and then showed me her sparkly engagement ring from Rod. The two were clearly in love and I was really happy for her but I wondered a) How did they keep their sex drive under wraps, and

b) would sex actually come up to their expectations when, after such a long drawn out courtship, they were let loose on each other?

Life went on, but we were chronically short of money. In truth, though I loved Tommy to bits I was getting a bit bored being at home all the time.

So when he was two and a half, I put him in a Nursery and found a part-time job at a local hairdressers.

My job was to wash the clients hair before the cuts, bring them tea/coffee and sweep up their unwanted locks. Apart from the minimum wage, I could keep any tips, and I would be taught to cut and colour, time permitting.

Irene of 'Irene's Salon' found me to be a good worker. Apparently, she had got though quite a few teenage girls, who didn't come up to scratch, so she had decided to plump for a 'more mature' lady. I didn't feel mature and I certainly wasn't a lady, but I did try to act like one, remembering Kathy's tuition.

The wages were low, but that was made up by some quite generous tips from the clients, especially if they liked the way Irene had styled their hair.

The atmosphere at the salon was great. There were two other girls working for the boss, Liz and Daphne and when the punters were in short supply and business was slow, we did each other's hair, read last months magazines and had a good giggle, all backed by 'pop' music streaming from the local radio station, which played all day to keep us bright and cheerful. Altogether a much better place to be than working at the Chemist shop, or staying home alone. Tommy was a smashing child, and I loved him dearly, but he was no substitute for adult company. I think he was probably happier playing with his little pals at the nursery too, rather than dragging round the supermarket with me, or being shouted to get out of the way, whilst I hovered the flat.

After a couple of weeks at the salon, I started to look at myself afresh, and compare myself, critically with the girls at work and some of the younger clients. On the whole my reflection was pleasing. The rather chubby face of my teenage years had definitely slimmed down and somehow my teeth didn't look so prominent. My features had become more chiselled, and my neck looked longer. My figure was now slimmer than before I'd had Tommy as all my puppy fat had been driven away by house work, childcare ,and making ends meet and last but not least, lots of hot sex! However tired we were, our sex life flourished!

Food had definitely taken a back seat in my life.

I looked again at my image in the mirror . I was looking a little bit more like my role model, Kathy, and yet, not completely. What was wrong? Somehow I wasn't satisfied with what I saw, and the more I looked the less satisfied I felt. So when Terry got home from work, I asked him if he still thought I was attractive.

"God yes!" he said "you're beautiful" I was pleased with his enthusiasm, but I still hated it when he used God's name in vain, despite my ambivalence about religion. In my heart of hearts, I knew, by his behaviour in bed, that he fancied me rotten, but dwelling on it, I realised our love-making was now always in the dark, so as not to disturb Tommy whose cot was in our one room. It struck me that my husband hadn't seen me naked for ages. Perhaps all the time we were having sex he was fantasising about was one of the celebrities he saw on TV. I was working myself up into a state.

"Look" he said when he saw me looking worried, "Let's have tea, Pet, I'm starved! Then we can talk about anything you like."

He was **so** nice, so normal, and so good for me, making me feel almost normal, myself. And here was I becoming obsessed with my appearance, while the man I loved accepted me as I was, and liked it.

But I was becoming obsessed, not in a celebrity way, but in a fearful way, of 'looking wrong', not being the 'right' shape, the 'normal' shape and it was starting to frighten me. I started checking myself in the mirror, several times a day, at work not to appreciate my slimmer figure, or my new hairstyle, but to pick faults with the reflection. Faults with the image, was that really me? How did other people see my face and figure? I could only see a copy of it in the glass, not the real me. The real me felt rubbish!

We did talk about it, after tea, and on many more evenings. Terry always said I looked fine...perfect to him, but I was never satisfied by his complements. He obviously had a vision of me, from day one and didn't see any down hill changes in me. What was he really thinking? Or was he getting bored and thinking of something else?

He was getting understandably irritated by my nightly cross-questioning, but I kept on at him. I was driven. I would interrogate him constantly by asking

"Are my boobs big enough?"

"Is my bum too big?"

"Do you think my legs look long enough?"

"Am I in proportion?"

Terry came home from work one night saying that his mate had seen a television programme about makeovers.

Apparently a prominent Chinese fashion mogul had started a show on one of the commercial channels in which ugly, fat, wrinkled and generally unattractive women, or as Terry said pointedly, those who **thought** they were, were given help and advice in every aspect of their looks, hair, skin, figure and choice of clothes. Eventually, at the end of several weeks of advice and material help, the show goes on air. Firstly, a poster of the 'new' woman, now looking like a celebrity, is paraded down the High street with shoppers and bystanders being asked if they think this woman is beautiful; (of course anyone who disagrees is edited out) and finally, at a great finale, the lady who's had the makeover walks down the cat-walk in her favourite outfit, among other real models, to huge applause. The finale consists of this same lady, the star of the show, walking down the catwalk, semi-naked, showing off her 'perfect' body to tumultuous applause! When Terry had finished describing this, in his usual hesitant way, interspersed with an occasional expletive, I laughed!

"So," he said, "That could be you!"

"I could never! How do you get on something like that?"

"I know you're gorgeous anyway, but think of it, you'd be famous, strutting down that cat-walk! I'd be so proud"

"Don't be ridiculous, Terry. I'd hate it and anyway they'd never chose me"

So he looked up the details and discovered that the show was still running. After the credits they asked for women to apply for next season's show.

Chapter 5

Strutting my stuff down the catwalk was exhilarating!

All I can remember was a sea of smiling faces, as I strode between the audience down the aisle in my beautiful, figure hugging dress wearing 5inch heels. Wow!! Was this really me!? It was like being a bride, walking down the aisle in the grand wedding I'd never had.

Out of the corner of my eye, I could see my two Ts, in the front row. Tommy sitting on his dad's knee, both craning their necks to look up at me, as I swished by. They were grinning and clapping their hands with pride, and ownership.

After this I was all aglow with excitement and amazement, had I really done what I had just done, or was it one of those dreams that turn into a nightmare. The sort of nightmare where no-one is who they pretend to be, and the stage turns into a catamaran, slowly sinking, ruining my new dress, which then rapidly turns into a sharkskin diving suit and but no one gives me a snorkel… No! I **had** walked the cat-walk. "Get a grip, Clarice" I said aloud, but not so loud that anyone else could hear.

Someone gave me a drink of water and I started to prepare for the finale. All the guys seemed very excited behind the scenes, but I felt a slight chill. How would my body be perceived after all these preparations. Everyone in the show from the producers down to my make-up artist had said, before hand, that I looked wonderful. I took off my dress and underwear, and put on the see-through body stocking, to lend some modesty to my very private parts. This was just in case the shimmering ribbons, which were to give the illusion of me being wrapped in a bandbox, fell off before time. My heart started to hammer.

I glided along the catwalk again, this time in crystal slippers. The applause, like drum rolls in my head, took me to another place. As I walked back towards the exit, all the ribbons were allowed to fall to the floor, and I was displayed as nude and as raw as the day I was born…I turned to let them to appreciate me from the rear, and then quickly disappeared from sight. Everyone was shouting "Great Stuff! You really wowed them, Clarice!" "Fantastic stuff" "Great show, girl, you really gave it to them"

Terry came back stage and a glass of Champagne was thrust into his hand by one of the crew, who was thumping him on the back. The others all joined in to congratulate him, "You've got a cracker there mate!" they said "She really did you proud!" The gay crew members showed their appreciation in a more genteel fashion. They were enchanted by my appearance, which was largely their own creation! One was Gavin, who had been my dresser and his friend was my hair stylist. They both looked like the cats who'd got the cream!

But we had to get back home,and leave them to continue to party. Tommy was getting restless and sleepy and Terry was slightly drunk, so it was lucky a cab had been booked to get us home. I was exhausted from the last few weeks of 'being made to feel better about myself.' These weeks had been great fun, but I'd kept on going in to do my shifts at the salon, and had not said a word about my re-make preparations to the other to the girls. I knew they all watched the show each week, but wondered what their reaction to seeing me on it, would be. So, after a weekend's R&R & doing boring old housework on Monday, as the salon was always shut, I went into work on Tuesday morning, expecting an amazing welcome. Little Miss 'Nobody', with the funny looking appearance, had made it on to television. Thanks to Terry, had made it onto one of the biggest and most popular reality shows, looking, apparently amazing. I knew the dress and those heels had made me look like a princess! After all, despite my reluctance to apply to go the show, in the first place and despite knowing, at the beginning that I looked awful; Thinking that my body was out of proportion and that nothing looked good on me. 'Knowing' that people were either disregarding me as sad, or staring at my ugliness, I had been made, for one single night of my life, to look beautifully in proportion, and actually, stunningly beautiful.

I walked into the shop on Tuesday morning waiting to see the surprise on their faces and their amazed response.

Clarice, 'From Cinders to the Prince's heart throb in one night!'

Nothing! No response. It was business as usual. Nobody said anything. I was mortified! That was the moment that I decided that I probably wouldn't be training as a hairdresser.

What I hadn't realised was that these sorts of program are filmed months in advance and then shown as a series later in the year.

Gradually all the excitement of the show drained away from me, and Terry stopped mentioning it. Life continued as before. I was allowed to keep the dress, but actually, having no grand functions to attend, it stayed, stored away under plastic in the depths of my wardrobe.

The following year, we were allotted a three bed-roomed council house. That was a break through! We had put our names down as soon as we had got married, because life in a tiny one bed roomed flat was hard, but with a tiddler, growing fast, we had worked out that it would fast become unbearable.

As soon as we moved in, we decided to convert the box room into a study; not that either of us was studious, but we wanted to get a computer. Then we could go on line and compare prices of all the goodies we couldn't afford, I could surf the net for 'Celebrity' news and Terry could play computer games in the evening. It would be perfect, and eventually, we thought, Tommy could use it for his home-work projects.

The house was in Debden and so I no longer lived just around the corner from the hairdresser's. Now I had to take the bus into work.

Tommy was starting proper school in the September, in Debden, so I could see logistic problems looming on the horizon.

I decided to look around locally for a new job. Perhaps something a little more taxing, now Tom was getting bigger.

The following week I checked in to the Willow Green Medical centre, the nearest doctors' surgery to our new home, with a view to seeing a nurse to get 'the pill'.

I had forgotten that red tape was running rings round the NHS, and that it was necessary to fill in a multitude of forms, and then go home to get identification, before they could sign me on as a new patient.

The Nurse was young-middle aged and chatty. She wore a maroon top over navy trousers and a badge, saying her name was Gloria...I thought this would have better suited Irene the Salon owner. Gloria took a brief history asking me about thrombosis, which I'd never had, and smoking, which I'd never done. My blood pressure was normal. I smiled.

'You'll love it here", she said "the staff are all really helpful and the doctors are all nice. Who have you registered with?"

I looked down at my new medical card, "Dr Fox, I think, what's he like?"

"He's a really nice old chap; our senior partner. You can't go wrong with him, and he's ever so good with kids."

"Thanks so much Gloria". I said "I'm completely new to this area and do want to get to know a bit more about it, but what with work and taking Tommy backwards and forwards to school, it's quite hard, time-wise."

"Where **do** you work, Clarice?" she asked.

"Well, at the moment I have to go by bus to Woodford. But I'm beginning to think it's too far without a car."

"Maybe you should think about looking for something more local, dear?"

"You're right, I should. There's so much to think about with the new house and everything. My husband said I should learn to drive. The thing is when to do what and in which order!"

As Clarice left the room, Gloria thought she recognised that face! Where had she seen it before? She racked her brains. There was a knock on the door and the hard working nurse, turned her attention to her next patient.

I carried on working, mornings only at the Salon. With help from some of the mums from school, we worked out at rota for taking turns at taking and picking up our respective children from school.

The salon was 30 minutes away by bus on a good day, that is when there were no hold-ups on the road and the bus was on time, and although I only worked four days a week plus Saturdays, (our busiest day) I was finding it all a bit much. Terry thought I was running myself ragged! He still left very early for work and was dead tired in the evenings. Everything seemed harder since we had moved, except that now we had room to expand.

"What about learning to drive now, Clarice?" Terry said one evening "You could use the van for work and I cold get Ron to pick me up."

So I started driving lessons which we could barely afford, with a driver from the BSM. He was an old guy, called Mr Davis, (we never did get onto first name terms) who didn't say much and was pretty restrained when I did ridiculous manoeuvres. It was as if I just couldn't concentrate on his instructions or put them into practice. There seemed to be a gap in my brain between being told what to do, and doing it. When I'd been taught other things I'd always coped, listening carefully and gradually perfecting most tasks. But not where driving was concerned, I could not co-ordinate my feet on the pedals, and would accelerate madly after being told to slow down. I would judder to a halt unexpectedly when the instructor was expecting me to drive smoothly, and it seemed as if he'd filled the car with 'kangaroo' petrol when I got in to drive! I couldn't back to save my life and three point turns were disastrous. I'd end up with my wheels firmly lodged against the kerb, quite unable to turn the steering wheel. So far we'd spent a long time going round and round the local disused airfield and then onto the very, very minor back roads where nobody much goes. Finally, on the third evening session, we were travelling along quite fast for me, when out of the corner of my eye I saw a cat looking as if it might shoot across the road. I slammed on the brakes and at the same time must have wrenched steering wheel hard down to the left. As we mounted the pavement I let out a scream and the car stopped dead. The cat watched, amazed, turned on his tail and leapt over the nearest garden wall.

Mr Davis who had obviously trained himself to remain calm under truly provoking circumstances, grunted, but said nothing. I on the other hand began crying hysterically, saying I could have killed us both, and refusing to drive another inch. I made him come round to the driver's side and take over from me, while I went round to the passenger seat. He drove me home.

"I'm not doing that any more" I announced to Terry that night I was still shaking a bit inside. "I've had it, I'm not cut out for driving, in fact, I'm positively dangerous. I can't face any more lessons and that's that!" I started to cry and Terry could see there was absolutely know point in arguing.

In bed that night, my brain was whirring. I couldn't just give up on work, we needed the money. In fact we were desperately short of cash, and Tom was getting more expensive by the day. Terry had no prospects and I just couldn't face juggling the unpredictable journey to the salon and childcare, any longer.

Next morning, I gave my notice in and the following week enrolled in a typing class at the local 6th form college. They told me it was free, but I'd have to rub shoulders with the six form students.

I wasn't an A* student myself, so that suited me fine... better than driving!

Within a term I was a semi-proficient typist, but not up to speed.

Every day I walked past the corner shop and glanced through all the ads. Nothing. I had been out of work for 4 months and money was getting very tight. Now I had time to care for my two men properly, cook meals, clean the house and chat to other mums at the school gate. An unexciting and poverty stricken life? Well not quite that bad.

Chapter 6

I took Tom down to the surgery for his pre-school booster. A bit late, as he had been at the school for two terms already. We should have been called in for it much earlier, but what with the house move to a new district, and change to a new Health Centre, things must have got a bit muddled up and delayed. That is the nature of things in this country. Millions spent on organisation, but precious little to show for it, at the patient's end of things. Shouldn't grumble though, at least kids were vaccinated in England, unlike the third world where we saw so many babies die of disease and starvation. Those TV documentaries broke my heart. Little kids on drips with gangs of flies settling round their eyes. Yes, we are lucky here, despite the odd glitch.

"Mum, why do we have to go? I'll be late for school and miss assembly. Our form is doing something for it this week. Miss Cook will be cross with me. I never told her I'd be late." I didn't know whether this worry was genuine, or Tom was really scared of jabs. He would never say if he was nervous, but he didn't seem to mind being late on normal days, always dragging his feet over breakfast, then disappearing upstairs for ages fiddling about.

"Muummm," he would shout "I'm only cleaning my teeth, like you said!"

"Well hurry up then. We're going to be late!" and I would hustle him into his duffle coat and check he'd tied his laces properly. He'd learnt really early to tie his laces, by making two loops and knotting these together, but sometimes they did undo themselves. And then I would rush him to school just as the bell was ringing.

Today he was anxiously nibbling at his nails. "Don't worry Tom, I'll write Miss Cook a note to explain why you're late and she'll be fine about it." He grunted and we walked on to school in silence, not holding hands, as we usually did. Tom still had his hands firmly in his pockets as we went through the big glass doors and up to the receptionist's desk at the Centre . "The nurse is running a bit late, dear, so take a seat, there's some comics and magazines on the table over there. She won't be too long." Said the woman behind the desk, who sounded really kind (and I had heard all receptionists were dragons!) In the middle of the seating area, there were some kids books and colouring books and crayons . Tom started to rummage through them and I went over to the notice board. There were the usual health reminders about smears and check-ups, but in the corner there was a notice headed, 'Posts available' 1) Health care worker, with some experience (in-post training given) 2) Part-time Receptionist (Typing desirable, but not essential)

My first thought was 'fantastic, could I fill the second bill?' Then I wondered why on earth they were advertising here in the Centre. Surely it would be better in some health or medical magazine. Would they allow somebody who was a patient work for them? What about confidentiality? Not my problem! I was about to jot down the details, when Tom's name was called out, by the nurse.

It wasn't Gloria. Apparently she majored in contraception and maternal health, while Celia did the jabs. She was nice and very young and kind of reminded me of myself when I looked after Lois and Jamie. She must be older than sixteen to be qualified, but she didn't look it.

"Hello, young man." She said, and Tom hung his head. He hated this jovial approach to what he considered basically, common assault. The jab must have been painless, though, as he didn't even flinch. We thanked Celia and went to go home; but the ad was big in my mind. That job could be a gift to me. I went over to reception, and was met by a smile and questioning look from the lady behind the desk.

"Can I help you at all?" she asked

"I felt a bit nervous but came straight out with my query, "I hope you don't mind me asking, but why are they advertising for a receptionist on the public board, like that?" That's a bit unusual isn't it?"

"Yes, I guess you're right, the last one left in a hurry! Gina! So sweet but couldn't really cope with the job, so now we're very short staffed. Another member of staff's away to, on long term sick leave, so we're pretty desperate at the moment. Are you interested? If so...she looked really hopeful...I'll tell the practice manager."

"Well, yes I am, **very** interested, but I need to get this boy back to school." I said looking down at Tom's ruffled hair.

"Look, I'll have a word with Di, our manager and see if she can make an appointment to see you later. Hang on a minute, I'll have a word."

She retreated into the inner sanctum and in a couple of minutes returned "Yes, Di could see you at 11am. Any good for you?"

Di welcomed me with "Thanks for coming along. It's desperate measures at the moment, I'm afraid"

"No, thank **you** for seeing me; since I moved here I've been trying to find a job, but didn't know where to look."

Di asked if I'd had any previous experience at reception work

"No, not as such, but I was a hair dresser, so I'm quite good with customers.

Boosting their morale is quite a big part of the business. They choose a hairstyle from a magazine, and don't understand when it doesn't look quite so good on them! I think they expect a model face to come with the hairstyle!"

Di laughed, "I can see you've got a good sense of humour, and you'll need it working here!" My turn to laugh!

"Of course I will need two references, before you can be considered."

"I can type as well!" I added

"Even better" said Di, "We have got a secretary, but it's always good to have a back up, otherwise I have to double up as typist!"

My heart was bumping against my ribs with excitement. I stood up to go, holding out my hand.

"Thank you so much for seeing me at short notice."

"I should be thanking you, Clarice. Leave your references at the desk, and if they're good, the job is yours!"

I could have kissed her!

Kathy and Irene could be depended on to write me glowing references! I hoped. No reason not to. I'd phone to warn them of the urgency. Should really have asked their permission first, I suppose, but somehow life doesn't work like that. When things come along, they come on you so quickly!

Working at Willow Green was definitely the best job I'd had, so far.

The money was fair, though, unfortunately the patients weren't allowed to give us tips for fitting us in with there favourite doctor!

The best thing was the camaraderie. All the girls got on together and welcomed me in as one of them, straight away. We chatted and giggled, grumbled about the management and rotas, discussed the doctors, not always favourably! But most of all we drank coffee and eat homemade cakes. Baking was Gloria's hobby. We liked that very much!

The shift system fitted my home life perfectly. In term, time I was always able to take Tom to school and my neighbour collected him. In the school holidays, I worked three evenings, after Terry got in from work. He'd taken to leaving unreasonably early to do this, but his mate agreed, better to start early, miss the rush hour, and get back for some evening. They were working on a huge enterprise for a firm in the East End, building a shopping Mall and then some 'assisted living' accommodation for the elderly, so his work was secure and plentiful for the time being. Now that I was in a safer part-time job money had ceased to be a problem at home and we could do more to the new house., and let Tom have more of the stuff his school friends had. Not that he was one of those acquisitive kids, always wanting something new and then as soon as they got it, nagging about the next 'must-have. ' Over the next two or three years, I felt the most settled I had ever been.

I got to know the foibles of all the Medical staff, who seemed to behave like strangers to us normal girls in the office! They were a group apart, and often acted like the group above. Whereas all the centre's lay staff including the nurses, worked as a team, the doctors each demanded individual treatment, and acted out if they weren't treated with kid gloves. I thought this attitude must have developed because patients hung on their words, and looked on them as demi-gods. But, like the rest of the girls, I found myself pandering to them as they were the Pay-masters. I didn't agree with it though, secretly I thought they should grow up, and get real!

Dr Fox, who'd originally been described to me by Gloria, as 'a nice old chap', was actually quite difficult. He acted like the elder Statesman, and, it seemed, he intended to hang on as long as possible, rather than make room for some younger colleagues. The patients adored him. He practised 'Olde Worlde' medicine, patronising the patients and sending them off with a hearty slap on the back and a bottle of his 'special' jollop. Amazingly, most of them got better, perhaps because there had been nothing much wrong with them in the first place. His old regulars could never be persuaded to see any other doctor.

The younger three were resigned to his dated approach, and accepted, that while Dr Fox remained, change would have to wait.

Nevertheless, they got the Practice Manager to try to teach him how to use the computer, which had become essential with Government changes.

The other three doctors learnt to use the computers for consultations and prescriptions, the nurses used them to check whether Imms and Smears were up to date, and we in reception used them for booking in patients and checking lab results. Dr Fox continued with the old style files and wrote his prescriptions by hand!

The day Dr Fox announced that he could no longer manage home visits, especially the evening ones, his younger counterparts raised the flag!

This was their chance to politely force him into a back seat and each grab a piece of his power. When he finally took 24hour retirement, he returned to find his name had been removed from the top of the list of the four doctors on the headed note paper and placed at the bottom. He was not amused.

Drs Thorpe, Evans & Cosgrove, or as they wished us to call us, James, Felicity and Charlie, took charge. This first name thing was seen as their attempt to be on a level playing field with the rest of us. Of course, that didn't work, because they earned so much more than us, and had medical degrees!

Charlie was the new boy, and so to avoid having his mistakes being picked up by his partners, he became obsessive; always checking everything himself, even things he had asked the receptionist to do, thus pissing us all off.

Felicity did all the women's medicine and saw most of the kids. She also specialised in 'Skins', which I thought was a good choice, as she could make the diagnosis without getting her hands dirty, by probing the depths!

There was no doubt James Thorpe fancied himself. He was charming to patients and staff alike, even chatting to us between surgeries. He would tell us stories about his wife, Ginny and about Muffin, his little dog, and outrageous tales about his twin boys at Uni. He seemed to like his family in that order, though sometimes it seemed that Muffin might have edged to the top of the list, ahead of Ginny.

I rated him nice but egoistic. To be fair, he did remember every one of the staff's birthdays with a card and flowers. I guess he had a little book.

Leading off the main reception were a number of little rooms, and it was in one of these, I sat doing my typing, when, Jean, the secretary was absent. Our paths rarely crossed.

James always had a mountain of typing. Apart from the run of the mill referral letters, he examined new employees for big firms, did DVLA and insurance medicals, and saw a handful of private patients. All these extra-NHS activities generated a mass of typing. To be fair to his partners, I thought that he should have employed a personal secretary. I wasn't sure if all the money from the 'other' work was shared out, but if it wasn't, he should definitely have paid for a private secretary; he made a tidy income on the side. Jean, the permanent secretary, did her best to cope, but there was always a stack of typing to wade through, on her free days, and that fell to me. Well, 'Overtime' I thought 'Can't be bad'. So I told Terry that I'd be late home more often than not, and he was quite happy playing video games with Tom.

One morning, James came into the typing den, "Hi Clarice," he said," I've brought you a cup of coffee. You put in so many hours with all this wretched typing, I thought you might be getting thirsty."" 'Yes' I thought 'Your wretched typing' But I smiled. No sense in biting the hand that fed me.

He chatted about the football at the weekend, but when he saw me de-focus, he went on to talk about the Sunday night quiz night, that he and Ginny went to, every Sunday night. Apparently, his team often won! Why was I not surprised? He asked me a few of the questions he had obviously got right. I hadn't a clue, but he was my boss, and I pretended to look interested. "Maybe you and your husband would like to come with Ginny and me one evening. See if you can help us win!?"

"I'd really like, that but we can't leave our boy on his own, he's too young."

"Okay. Just a thought." He said.

I didn't mention it to Terry.

Two years after I started work at 'Willow', the secretary, Jean, left to have a baby.

Di approached me, "Clarice, how would you like to be our full time secretary, while Jean's away on maternity leave? You've been doing so much extra recently, filling in for her, when she's been off sick. I've asked the doctors and they've all been very pleased with your work. They suggested I asked you"

"Thanks Di," I said "I'd like that a lot." Not having to work on reception meant even more elasticity where Tom was concerned, I could more or less fit my hours round him. Also, I knew Terry would be pleased with any extra money that came our way. "Will I get more money? Or are all the staff paid the same?"

"The pay rate's the same, I'm afraid," said Di "but there should be more overtime, if you're interested. And off course, we'll have to keep the job open for Jean when she comes back after the baby."

'Oh well,' I thought to myself 'she might never come back!'

I couldn't wait to tell Terry that night. I danced round the room, singing 'I'm a secretary bird, I'm a secretary bird! Hurray!!' Tom, doing his home work in the corner, winced.

After that, all the partners loaded me up with work. I always managed to get through it all even if it meant staying after most of the staff had gone home. Felicity used to leave when she had finished seeing all her patients and cleared her in-tray. She was definitely the most efficient of the doctors. Obsession and fear of making any mistakes made Charlie check and recheck his computer, going over his consultations, to be quite sure he had left nothing undone, so he left next, looking worn out and worried as usual.

Dr Fox only did mornings now, so I hardly saw him and James usually made me a cup of coffee, before rushing off to one of the many meetings GPs had to attend. So only the cleaners and I carried on into the late evening, when the Medical Centre, busy and noisy by day, had emptied and become a virtual ghost town.

Out of the blue, I had a phone call from Di., on my free day.

Could I come in and do some extra hours, urgently?

"Why, what's happened, Di?"

"It's James,he's collapsed!" she replied

"How? What happened?" I asked

"He was on his way back home to lunch and collapsed at the wheel of his car! Luckily the pains made him pull over, so no-one was injured."

"Where is he now?"

"In Coronary care."

"Oh I'm so sorry . Does his wife know" I asked

"Not sure ." said Di, We're going to send him a get-well card. I don't think flowers are allowed in CCU."

"Oh, I'm so sorry," I repeated "Of course, I'll help, I'll do whatever I can."

"Thanks dear," said Di "Its just that we found lots of work in his in-tray ready to be typed . I want to make sure everything is kept up to date, so when he gets back, he won't feel flustered." Quite," I said, not that I could ever see James flustered. 'Quite a cool character.' I thought, 'But maybe the heart attack, if that's what it was, showed he took the stress inside?'

When I'd checked through all his outstanding non-NHS work, I phoned the insurance companies to explain why Dr Thorpe hadn't been able to examine all the candidates they had requested. I explained that other partners in the practice could take these over, if they were happy with this. Then,

I typed all the letters left on his recording machine and at lunch-time, went out and bought a 'get-well soon' card from the corner shop.

I pondered. James had looked so well, before the event. So men, in their prime, apparently healthy, really could be brought down by some sinister internal malfunction deep inside, which, without them knowing gathered momentum, till finally it struck.

I thought of Terry. He was nearing the dangerous age. He was thin and wiry though and had given up smoking ages ago. I never thought of Terry as getting ill. If I had thought about the future at all, I would have fondly imagined that we would live happily on into old age. A typical 'Derby and Joan' with Tom and his wife living nearby and our grand- kid's, popping round to run errands for a few bob!? No! Of course not, that was an old-fashioned idea! Where had I got it from? It hadn't been true of my Mum and Dad, had it? I realised I hadn't phoned Mum for months. And when I had I'd never really listened to her moans about Dad & Trevor. I just couldn't bear to go back and think of that life. Now I started to worry about Terry, he was never ill, but unexpected things happened, with no warning. I would try and persuade him to have a 'Well man check-up'

That night I held him very tightly, till I dozed into a fitful sleep.

James returned to work six weeks later. He had lost weight and looked fitter.

He said that he now realised life was too short for all the things he wanted to do. After his return to work, he made a point of having a coffee break with me at least once a week. He said I made him feel calmer! I don't know why, because I have always been in turmoil inside. I probably hide it well!

"Life slips away, Clarice" he said, "Without us ever logging it" He said that the heart attack had shown him that he took life too seriously and now he had make up his mind to have more fun, and take on less extra work. "What is money, compared to life?" he mused

'He'd obviously never been poor!" I thought.

There was no reduction in the amount of typing, but I noticed James sloped off early more often than before. He took days off to go to Cricket at Lords, up to London to Shows, took Ginny to see their boys. All this he told me at coffee in the little room.

Then there were the exotic holidays, in Mauritius, cricket in the West Indies, Scuba diving in the Maldives "you can't take your tops off there, girls!" he told the staff as he handed round his photos for us all to coo over.

He regaled us all with descriptions of the journeys, dancing on the beaches to the sound of drums and, most of all, the food. The foreign delicacies and exotic dishes. He immediately caught my attention when he started to eulogise over food. He did all the cooking at home, because Ginny was a picky eater and couldn't be bothered in the kitchen.

It was on an Autumn day of the third year of my employment at Willow Green, that things changed.

It was blustery outside, so the first thing I did when I got in, was go to the ladies' cloakroom and comb my hair. I stared at myself in the mirror. My face had aged pleasantly, not too many lines, and I looked more a woman of the world, but, deep down beneath that artefact, lived the same timid, unsure girl, with a hundred hang-ups, that was the real Clarice. I knew her so well!

I said "Hi" to the girls in reception and, as usual everyone seemed in a good mood. It was great that we got on so well. The name Gina flashed through my mind. I wondered why she had left so suddenly? Family problems? Boyfriend troubles? No one mentioned her. Never mind, thanks to her I had a great job.

When I got to the typing room a huge pile of typing had appeared, though I had almost cleared the backlog. 'Oh well, nevermind,'I thought "At least I'm becoming indispensable!"

I didn't see at first, but behind the pile of accumulated work was a large box of Black Magic chocolates, and beside them a small bunch of pale yellow freesias! Where ever had they come from? I automatically put the freesias to my nose, people said that they had a beautiful perfume, but I still couldn't smell them, being one of the small percentage of people who haven't got the right receptors. Still they looked lovely.

There was a tiny card, hidden among the flowers.

It said, 'To my Special secretary, to thank you for all your hard work, James x'

It was a wonderful thank you. I was charmed. It was true, I had worked really hard while he was on sick leave, but that was sometime ago, and I **was** being paid!

I went over to the list of phone and mobile numbers pinned behind the reception desk and tapped James's number into my 'phone.

'Hi James thanx a mill 4 pressys. Y tho? I do get paid (smiley face) C x'

I debated about putting the 'x', deleting and re-adding it several times. Hey ho he sent me one and I text it to all my mates.

The message came back in a flash! 'In the sun @ Rose Bowl, thinkin of u'

I asked immediately 'Hv u bin drinkin?'

'In vino veritas' James replied!

I thought I knew what it meant, but I Googled it to check, in case I'd got it wrong.

'In wine there is truth' was one translation, another was more long winded 'A Latin expression meaning that when you drink alcohol you sometimes say things that you wouldn't say had you not imbibed.'

Golly! I wish I hadn't looked it up. I felt more muddled now. Best to let sleeping dogs lie. I knew the meaning of that saying!

When Terry came in that night and saw the flowers, he asked where I'd got them from. I simply said "Grateful patient!" but he had already turned on the TV to watch the Snooker.

That was the beginning.

Chapter 7

On Saturday, Terry drove me to the supermarket, to do the usual big weekly shop, while Tom went to play with his friend Stevie over the road. There was nothing Tom hated more than dragging round shops, after us. Terry pushed the trolley and I picked the items. It was always the same routine, I chose food for the week's suppers first, always avoiding 'ready meals', because you never knew what rubbish they put in them. Ever since working for Kathy, I'd continued to cook from first principles, and it was one of my favourite chores. Crisps and twiglets, were next on the list, to go in the lads lunchtime sandwich boxes. Then I picked out the boring house-hold necessities, and then, at last we reached the treats! Always the same, chocolate for Tom, savouries, like gerkins and olives, for Terry and pastries for me. I chose my treats very carefully, and then when, Terry was looking the other way, I slipped in some more. Mini frozen éclairs, this time, I was particularly addicted to them! Not that Terry would have minded, or tried to stop me buying them, but a girl's got to keep some things to herself! No need to buy any biscuits, though, Di, bought hordes of these at the Health Centre to 'keep us going'!

Last of all, near the check-out, some beers for Terry. I always took him out a pick-me-up after he'd mowed our little patch of lawn, tidied up the flower beds and watered the hanging baskets. Gardening was Terry's new hobby. Last spring he had planted out some glorious hanging baskets with trailing geraniums and lobelia. They brightened up the back of the house, a treat. He'd watered them with a specially adapted long-spouted watering can. Next year he was planning to make a little pond surrounded by reeds and populated with Koi carp, for Tom to feed. He'd seen the idea on TV and his work mate, Ron had already constructed one at home and his wife was thrilled. The garden was Terry's weekend hobby and he loved to dig it and water. He loved choosing new plants and putting them in and keeping the grass cut smartly, but his proudest moment was when I came out from the house, with his can of lager, to admire his handiwork.

"Wow! that's fantastic, Terry" I would say, as he showed me his latest acquisition."

"Well, pet, I do love the fresh air and working the soil, but what I like best is making it nice for you! What do you think I should put in the hanging baskets this summer?"

While Terry was in charge of the garden, it was my greatest pleasure to take over the kitchen, and food. So we were both well pleased with our respective 'hobbies'. As I said, no ready meals! Instead I indulged my men-folk with luscious soups and casseroles, roasts and pies, and cakes and puddings. Needless to say, they downed them all with relish! Tom was no fussy eater like my brother, thank goodness! Sometimes I wondered where they put it all, because no matter how much they eat, they never got fat. I suppose Tom was growing taller as I watched, and Terry must have used it up doing such an energetic job. They were both always starving when they got in.

The three of us had such a happy home together, and now, with enough money coming in to make us comfortable, my stress levels had fallen, so eating for me had taken a back seat,... accept, of course, for the occasional, naughty little cream cake I slipped down, while I was cooking 'Well,' I Thought, 'chefs on telly often swig a glass of sherry while they cook! But I prefer a tasty cream cake, or two, to nibble.' Old habits die hard.

That evening when Tom was upstairs in his room, playing a video game, Terry started to wax eloquent. It was unusual for him to chat like this, normally a man of very few words.

He snuggled up to me and said "Clarice have you ever thought how lucky we are?"

"Yes." I said, "Funnily enough, I was thinking just the same, earlier on while I was getting the tea."

"We should count our blessings more often," he continued "We've got a lovely kid, a nice home and we've stuck together!"

"Hhmmm" I murmured." "Clarice, d'ya remember that day you strode down that catwalk with nothing on but ribbons?" I smiled and he continued "I knew then that every man in that audience envied me sick, 'cos I **had** what was underneath those ribbons!" With that I felt his cock rise against my thigh, and I felt my wetness. We started petting and giggling, on the sofa, but we soon slipped to the floor. Terry's kisses were 'to die for', and I was soon weakly helpless in his arms. He lifted my shift and entered me there and then. He thrust hard and fast, till at last with a gasp, we climaxed together.

The noise of Tom, sliding down the banisters made us jump to attention, instantly. For the first time in our married life, we'd forgotten about Tom! He didn't come into the living room, thank goodness, but we heard him go straight into the kitchen to get some cereal. "I'm just going to bed now, Mum" he called out as he went back upstairs.

As soon as we got into bed I noticed Terry was hard again. He turned to me, "Clarice," he said, "I am the luckiest man alive." and then made the most passionate love to me, since our courting days. I came for the second time that night, and then I fell into a deep and dreamless sex- induced sleep, in the arms of the man that I loved.

Tom bounded into our bedroom on Sunday morning and jumped straight onto our bed, despite the fact he was now verging on double figures.

"Come on, it's late! You've overslept" he shouted right in my ear.

"You make me get up early every morning in the week for school, which I hate and now, you can get up for me!" He squashed uncomfortably in between us.

"Remember what you said? If it's nice we'll go to Southend today.

Can we take a picnic for the beach?"

Had we said that? I was still dazed from my sex induced coma to remember anything very clearly.

But we did get a move on. Seeing his toothy grin reminded me of how I had felt as a child. That helpless feeling of seeing my Dad's immobile body lying on the couch, recovering from the previous night's excesses.

We had some tea and toast. Tom cleaned his teeth without being asked and then started to help Terry make some sandwiches. The two of them concocted some lopsided sarnies, some with ham and some with tuna, and then took the van to the local shops to get some cola and comics to read on the beach and an 'Elle' magazine for me.

When they came back Terry said "I flipped through this magazine on the stand, to see if it was your sort of thing, and it's full of beautiful women, but none of them are a patch on you, pet! You're what I call a real looker!"

I knew he was biased, but I also knew I was the luckiest woman alive!

We chased down the A12 in double quick time, beating the other day trippers who'd overslept.

My two boys spent the morning building a complicated waterway system in the sand. Although Tom was getting a bit old for this, Terry certainly wasn't and acted his shoe size. You'd never guess he was in his forties, and he had his hair **and** no beer gut. I thought again how lucky I was!

The two had a real team-building time, and I noticed how alike they looked, with the same hazel coloured eyes and open, slightly freckled faces, laughing and egging each other on, running up and down the beach, endlessly filling up buckets with sea water for the sand to suck away. Briefly, I thought how different their relationship was, from the one between my own dad and **his** son! But soon, the magazine I was flicking though slipped off my lap and I drifted off to sleep, in the sun shine.

After the picnic we all went down for a swim, though as always in Southend, it turned out to be more of a paddle: We did actually manage to lie down in the shallow water, which although rather muddy was soothingly warm, having come in over the sun-scorched sand.

The tide was coming in, and this time we noticed!

This day with Tom, was just as joyous as our honeymoon, but in a different way. Who would have guessed, at the outset of our marriage, that our little trio would be playing so happily together, so many years after that rather inauspicious start?

We wound up the day, sitting on the prom, eating a fish and chip supper washed down with mugs of hot tea, watching a surreal sunset.

It had been a perfect day.

Lying in bed that night, sunburnt and with sand still clinging to the skin between my toes, I thought 'That's how childhood should be.' Tom went up to bed, tired from the day and we soon followed, falling asleep, holding hands, too tired even to kiss.

It wasn't till the next morning, when I got into work, that I remembered the texts and shivered.

I shouldn't have worried though, as James was at a conference in Cambridge all week, and when he returned to Willow Green, he was his normal, friendly self. He came to see me in my little typing room, about once a week, usually on a Monday, to check over reports with me. He always brought in two cups of coffee and after the briefing, he'd ask me how my weekend had been. He told me snippets about his life and I always showed a friendly interest, but he rarely delved into mine. That was how I liked it. We became friends, though there was always something of the boss versus employee about the relationship. It was my year for friendships! I started to get on really well with a couple of the girls in the office, who had seemed cut off from me before, while I had been struggling with the new typing job. Their names were Nicole and Lara. Both were warm and chatty, but very different. In fact we were all different from each other and outside of work, we would probably never have crossed paths.

Nicole was sporty with a capital S. Though maybe it was a front she put on, so as to keep up with her family. Her three boys, now in their late teens and early twenties, were mad keen on football and supported West Ham. Her daughter played basket ball at county level. Listening to Nicole over the time I got to know her, I believe most of her alleged enthusiasm for sport was second hand, as she sat watching matches from the sidelines or on TV. She hadn't got the muscles or body shape off anyone who actually played, though she would have loved us all to think differently.

The whole family were going skiing after Christmas, and she would look good in a chunky sweater and woolly hat. I could see her clearly dressed like this, in my mind's eye, but I couldn't quite imagine her zipping down the piste at high speed.

When we could drag Lara away from 'Face Book' or looking for a bargain on eBay, she would joined in our girly chats. Lara came over as a happy-go-lucky young girl, though this was far from the truth. She was fat (No! 'Fat' is a swear word in my dictionary,) plump describes her better. She always covered her acne with layers of foundation, but never minded exposing her ample young bosom by wearing T-shirts, with low-scooped neck lines.

So we three often giggled together over the different things that tickled us. The way the doctors really disliked each other, while pretending that they were best buddies. The way they tried to shield us, and the rest of the work force, from their petty arguments. "All a question of professional jealousy" we heard Gloria say…and we sniggered. The way some of the patients moaned if they couldn't get to see their favourite doctor.

"We are all trained to the same level of knowledge" We had heard Dr Fox say… and we giggled again, because we knew it didn't work like that. Patients wanted to consult with the GP who suited them, and that was the end of story.

But, one day, in the rest room, which was usually deserted, Lara found me. She wasn't giggling anymore. Her life-story had been one long sob. Her father beat her brother regularly, and, when she thought he was going to start on her, she left home. She got pregnant by a lout, and so she felt she had no alternative than to have an abortion at seventeen. After that she started drinking, moved in with a slob of a boyfriend and now, because he was such a no-hoper, she had started to drink more. She told me that her Sundays always passed in a drunken daze.

She asked my advice. What should she should do?

What help could I possibly give her? Jo and her Church had saved my skin, but what state was I in now? Sometimes I felt confident and OK. When I was with Terry, I felt secure. But how was I really deep down inside? Was I an accident waiting to happen?

The only way I could help Lara was to be her friend. So, what did I say? I probably made the worst suggestion I could.

"Lara, how would you like to meet up for a drink, one evening after work?"

"Oh, I'd love to Clarice! Thanks for asking. Where shall we meet? What about asking Nicole to join us?"

'The Farmer's Arms' sounded a welcoming pub, and was only just across from the Heath Centre.

I was very glad that Nicole could join us that first evening. I felt she brought gravitas to the occasion, plus I had an idea that Lara wouldn't open up in front of her, in quite the same way as if we'd been alone.

I was right, Lara gave nothing away, and we had a great time; laughing and joking about shows we had seen on TV; what we would do if we won the lottery; should we start a syndicate at work? Nicole thought this would be a great idea, and would obviously give us a better chance of winning.

After a while, the alcohol kicked in and we laughed at nothing, nothing I can remember anyway. The taxi we had ordered for 10.30 arrived and dropped me off round the corner, continuing on with the other two.

"That was a really good evening." I told Terry when I got in. He shook himself out of his fireside snooze and we went up to bed together

When our trio worked together again that week, we all agreed to make the pub evening a regular event. We settled on once a month, mainly because of the cost; the last Friday in the month, after pay day.

Terry said he was pleased I'd made some more friends, knowing I sometimes missed the comaraderie of the salon.

The Christmas party was announced.

No partners allowed! And that applied to the doctors as well as staff.

It was held early in December, to avoid the rush, and was more of a dinner, than a party. The usual; we all sat round an oblong table and pulled crackers, read our mottos and wore funny hats. The alcohol flowed freely, and as Terry was picking me up afterwards, I didn't hold back. Another firm was holding their party at the same time, and we heard loud 'Guffaws' over the sexy 'Secret Santa' presents that they were opening.

Di, our practice Manager, had thought it would be unseemly for a medical practice to display such vulgarity! I sort of agreed with her. Some of our patients might see us and lose the little respect they had!

Afterwards, there was disco dancing in a room off the dining area, and all of us girls went to have a shimmy. None of the doctors followed, except James, who was dragged to his feet by the busty Lara. He looked a bit sheepish and sidled away as soon as he thought he politely could.

Terry popped his head round the door of the restaurant at the agreed time of 11.30pm and whisked me away like Cinderella, but well before the witching hour!

I asked Mum and Dad and my sibs down for Christmas Day, at Terry's insistence. "It'd be nice for them to meet Tom at last. He's your Mum's only grand child, you know?" I did know and he asked rhetorically. For years he'd nagged me to go and see the family rather than 'phone and send photos. Terry had lost touch with his own dad long ago and his mother had died before we met.

After much nagging, I rang to invite them. Mum was quite touched.

"No" she said "It's much to much for you. Besides Prue's more or less engaged to Phil now, so we'd have to bring him as well. Why don't you come to us?"

After shouting an exchange between Terry, who hated using the phone, and my Mum, it was agreed that we would drive up Chester, to see them.

It meant going on the motorway, which Terry also hated, especially at Christmas, but we decided to leave very early to miss the rush.

"Oh no" said Tom when he heard, "I want to be here for Christmas day like usual and open my presents round the tree, and help Dad make the dinner, just like I always do."

"Calm down, lad." said his Dad, "you've never met your Nan and Grandad!"

"Well, they've never bothered with me before." said Tom.

"That's not quite true, Tom" I interrupted. "They always remember your birthday and send you money at Christmas. I agree with your Dad, we ought to go. It's not like we live in Australia. Then we couldn't go to see them."

"What's Australia got to do with it?" Shouted Tom, "I don't want to go, and that's that!"

"I won't have you shout at your Mother, so be quiet. We are going, there's no argument about it."

Tom looked furious, but knew when he was beaten.

I didn't say anything, but I was already getting butterflies in my stomach at the thought of the reunion.

We set off early on Christmas Day, taking some chocolates and fizzy wine and crackers, as presents. Terry had thought that they might have preferred beers, but the wine looked more festive. Tom sat in the back of the car, plugged into his new ipod. To appease him, we had let him open his presents on Christmas Eve. "Like they do in Norway" I said but wasn't quite sure if I'd got the country right, but so what, if it made Tom was happy?

It seemed funny going home after so long. I had mixed feelings, but by the time we knocked at Mum's door, my heart was in my mouth.

The door was opened by a tall good-looking young lad, who I immediately took to be Prue's boyfriend.

"Hi Sis!" he said giving me a big hug "I've missed you!"

Was this really 'little' Trevor? I couldn't believe it. He was still on the wiry side, but so handsome. I could never have believed he would turn out like that in a million years! I introduced him to Terry and Tom. Tom grinned widely and I caught the family likeness. The three Ts together at last! Well it was a good home-coming. Then it was made even better by seeing Mum!

Mum in her flowery apron, smiling widely and giving off a smell of frying sausages and sage and onion, all mixed up. We hugged for almost the first time in living memory. The young couple were sitting on the sofa in the living room, all over each other. Prue had blossomed into a beautiful young woman, but her boyfriend Phil was less impressive, still having spots left over from adolescence and long rather greasy, black hair. He didn't say much but seemed okay, just too engrossed in my sister.

Christmas dinner was early. Mum had been slaving since dawn.

We all sat round the table and started to pull the crackers; but where was Dad?

There weren't enough places laid at the table. Only seven!

We all sat down and Mum started to carve the bird.

Possibilities were whirling round my mind. Was he upstairs, sleeping it off? Had there been a row? Had he stormed out and gone round to one of his drinking buddies? Surely not on Christmas Day!

"Mum, I started "Where's Dad going to sit?"

"Oh, he'll have his, sitting in the armchair. I'll just finish carving then we'll get him down." Mum said and then continued quickly, before I could ask more questions. "Come on all of you, help yourselves to veg,. Prue, could you pass the gravy round." She hardly stopped for breath, I could see she was very flustered.

"Trev, you open the Cava, there a good lad" she smiled at him.

Trevor immediately went out to the kitchen to get the bottles from the fridge. He gripped the first one between his legs and carefully unwound the wire with his hand, aiming the cork at the door. It gave a magnificent explosion as it popped out, and he quickly filled the first few glasses and then, when it ran out, he started on the second bottle. This cork was stiffer than the first. He tried to loosen it with his right hand, while steadying it with his left. Eventually he gave up, and passed it over for Phil to do the honours.

Trevor was blushing scarlet. He might be tall and handsome but still his disfigured left hand let him down. I looked away.

When we'd all been served Mum's delicious dinner, and most people had started to tuck in, I asked her again where Dad's was.

"I've put his on a plate to keep warm and I'll give it to him when we've finished." Mum looked down, concentrating on her food, avoiding my questioning stare.

Well I wasn't going to be the one to upset proceedings today. Everyone was getting on so well and Tom was in his element, chatting away with is new- found family. Terry had even let him have a small glass of bubbly. He was happy as Larry!

"Perhaps it was better without Dad, he'd always cast a cloud over things in the past. I tried to put memories of his alcohol fuelled rages out of my mind. This wasn't the time or place to muse!

"So Prue? Where are you working now?" I asked "Mum told me you'd been helping out at the stables."

"Yes, that's where I met Phil" she said, turning to give him one of her sunniest smiles.

'Oh, that fits,' I thought cattily, 'looks as if he does a lot of mucking out!'

"But I've left there now. Got a job at the Vet's, I'm training as a kennel maid. An apprenticeship like."

"Wow, Prue, I just can't believe how quickly you've grown up and how well you're doing! Just look at you! And nearly engaged? Mum said." I noticed Phil look down. "Well Clarice, it's years since we've set eyes on you." Answered Prue, "We all change, you know".

I wondered whether to whisper to her about, my concerns over Dad? Ask what was happening? Where was he? But she'd already turned back to Phil and was looking longingly into his rather deep-set, piggy eyes!

Mum stood up and started to clear the table.

"Mum, where **is** Dad?" I said. Everyone stared down at the cloth except my two Ts.

Her face went blank "I'll go and get him now, Clarice. Give us a hand would you, Trev?"

Prue plumped up the cushions in his chair, in readiness.

The man they helped slowly down the stairs was unrecognizable as my Father. Dressed in baggy old clothes and slippers, with dribble hanging out of the corner of his mouth, he dragged his feet slowly across the carpet to the chair. They manoeuvred him round, and he sat heavily down on the cushions. "Dad" I said he mumbled something under his breath. I went over to him. "It's Clarice, Dad. I've come to see you." His eyes showed no sign of recognition.

"Mum," I half-shouted, "What's wrong with him? How long has he been like this? You never said anything!"

"You haven't been in touch that much" she said "I didn't want to worry you, you've got enough on your plate, with the youngster and your important job at the Health Centre."

"Mum! It's not **that** important, I'm only a secretary. You should have told me. I had a right to know. What's happened to him? Did he have a stroke?"

"Let me just cut up his dinner and feed him then he'll nod off for a bit, and we can talk."

She wrapped a towel found his front to catch he drips, just like I had done to Tom when he was a baby. That's what Dad had become. He had become a child again in the guise of an old man, a sad, decrepit, pitiful old man. There was no 'father' left in him to fear, nor to mourn.

Pre-senile dementia the doctors said. He hadn't had a stroke, his present state had just crept up on him unawares, and his family were left to nurture his shell.

Mum said she hadn't noticed much of a change in him at first, though he hadn't wanted to get up for work some days, and more and more often forgot his packed lunch or his keys. She realised something was very wrong with him when he didn't want to go down to the pub any more. Said he felt too cold to walk the short distance there. Said he couldn't bear all that talking, it got on his nerves. Then one day, when he absolutely refused to leave his bed. She called in the GP.

Blood tests, memory tests and brain scans followed. His brain was shrinking, speeded by his heavy drinking. There was no cure. He refused to go into respite or have anyone but family near him. Mum was stuck permanently caring for a speechless invalid, whom she had ceased to love decades before.

'Poor cow' I thought, 'she doesn't deserve this. Nobody does!'

"It was lovely to see you, dear," Mum said as we left "Don't make it so long next time. Keep in touch" They all stood round the door, with it's back ground of bright lights, holly, and tinsel, glossily covering up the heart break in the living room.

In the car travelling home, Tom chatted about his Nan and his new found Auntie and Uncle. When can we see them again?" he asked and before we could think of an answer, mercifully, he plugged into his ipod.

"So that was Christmas…" said Terry as we trudged up to bed.

Chapter 8

On return to work, Di met me with the good news that Jean wanted to stay at home with her baby for another year, so she would not be returning to Willow Green for quite a while, if at all.

'Whoopee!' I thought, much preferring typing to reception work.

Apart from that piece of good news, the first couple of weeks back at work were dull like the weather. Because of the freezing, foggy mornings leading to sleety afternoons, the patients came in by their droves with Christmas coughs and colds. Miseries on two legs, poor things. I could hear it all from the safety of my little room. I was thankful not to be in the firing line of all their showers of germs and sometimes their hurled abuse, if they couldn't get an appointment pronto!

It was so drear, that Nic, Lara and I decided that, instead of waiting till pay-day to meet up for our next get-together, we would meet up on the coming Friday, despite funds running rather low.

We shivered as we walked the few hundred yards to the pub. The landlord recognised us immediately and put another huge log on the already roaring fire. The warmth from that and the first few sips of the house red, quickly warmed our cockles and loosened our tongues.

"Well, what **are** we going to do to make money?" started Lara, "I can't manage on what the what I get at the Health

Centre, and it doesn't look as if we're going to get a rise this year."

"Money's too tight!" said Nic, "Or **they** are! It's okay for the doctors! Have you seen how much they earn? I read it in the Sun."

And the Government's promised them a big increase if ·they get all their QOF points, whatever they are!"

"I might have to get a weekend job." Said Lara "I wonder if the Landlord would take me on? I certainly know my drinks!"

"Know how to hold your drinks!" I added. We all laughed and ordered another bottle of wine.

"What about the lottery?" I asked "We could form a syndicate. I'm sure some of the other girls would join in. Then we would get more chance of winning."

"Yes," said Nic "but less cash if we have to share it out."

"I've read somewhere that you may as well roll your pound coins down the drain, as play the lottery!" Said Lara

"But You know Ilford's a good place to win and that's right near us." I said The local taxi drivers got together and won millions." I tried to talk them round to giving It a go.

"But if there has already been a big win in this area, we would be less likely to win." countered Lara.

"No why? It doesn't work like that. They don't know where the winners live before hand. It's totally random."

By the third bottle of wine, I'd won them over. Nicole was elected to canvas the other girls in the office, so that we could enter the maximum number of lines each week.

After that I was £4 poorer each week, but...fingers crossed.

I began to really look forward to our coffee times together, James and I.

They had now become a regular fixture of my week. He said that I made him laugh, and that 'Cheering up Dr Thorpe' was going to be added to my job description. He said that the work load for doctors was getting heavier and more tedious, now they were having to collect more of patients' medical data, whether they were ill or not. It seemed crazy to him.

I agreed. I didn't mention the extra pay we all knew he and the partners would be getting for the added work. Somehow, it didn't seem my place to comment.

We were pals, James and I, and who said platonic friendships couldn't work? We **were** friends, but I knew it wasn't an equal relationship. He held the power.

By Easter, something had changed about the way he chatted to me. It was as if a new intimacy had developed, and I began to feel I had known him for a lifetime.

There were vibes; but only the kind you feel with a best girl friend or in the company of the family; those comfortable feelings of knowing and being known.

I told him that Terry loved doing the garden, all about his new pond and the hanging baskets he was going to replant in the summer.

James asked me if I was interested in gardening.

"No," I said "I just like looking. I leave all the work to Terry."

"Well then, Clarice," he said "how about you coming round to look at my garden and it might interest you, now the bulbs are starting to shoot. Ginny's done some brilliant spring planting this year. The snowdrops are over already, but the crocuses are out and all the daffs are in bud."

"I'd love to, James, but when? You're always working so hard and I haven't got a car."

"Don't worry. I can always make time for you. I'll pick you up one lunch hour. What about Thursday?"

"Yes. That'll be great!"

"About 12 o'clock Thursday then. It's a date!"

I thought about it afterwards. Of course when he said 'date' he have just meant an agreed time. What did he mean by 'I can always make time for you'? Was it my imagination or had his voice become just slightly sleazy.

'Don't be ridiculous, Clarice!' I said to myself, and to normalise it, I told Terry about the invitation as soon as he got home.

"That sounds nice, pet, "he said, "pick up some tips about bulb fibre from him, Ask him if it's really necessary or can I put our tulips straight in the soil. It would save a bit of time and money."

On Wednesday evening, I got a text from James. 'coffee, thurs @ 12 Jx'

There wasn't a question mark. It was definite. Why had I agreed? It seemed a good idea at the time. The fatal 'x' reminded me of a previous text! It scared me, but I wasn't sure why. I had a sinking feeling deep inside that I was about to risk sabotaging my happy home life. Smash the 'Crystal Ball'?

No! All I was going to do, was look at a handful of Spring flowers with a work colleague.

Jo 'phoned that night, a voice from the past. I'd sent out cards for the first time this last Christmas, including one to her with my new address and telephone number inside.

We chatted for a few minutes and then she said she had to go and prepare Rod's supper. She and Rod had finally married and he had been allowed to move into her flat, at last! She was expecting a baby in September. "How about we meet for lunch sometime soon? It would be nice to catch up."

"Yes" I said it would be great. "How about next Thursday? Not tomorrow, I'm afraid I'm busy with work."

I lied. Why did I lie, as if I had something to hide?

Anyway, I was becoming quite a socialite now with lunches lined up for two Thursdays running. Life was good and, I thought, about to get better.

But lunch wasn't on the menu for that first Thursday!

James picked me up from the end of the road "Mustn't make the other girls jealous!" he joked.

When we arrived at his house, which as one might expect, was very big, he took me in through the great, wooden front door. Then without a word, he led me through the hall and lounge, throwing open the French windows,as we went into the garden. He indicated the rustic seat which stood against the outside wall, surrounded by lush creepers not yet in flower, and said "Have a seat Clarice, and enjoy the view. I'm just going in to make us some coffee."

The crocuses were pretty and I could see the daffodils were about to break forth from bud, but I didn't think it was **that** wonderful, not like gardens of several Stately Homes we'd been round! And Terry had made our tiny garden just as lovely last summer, with his hanging baskets.

James came out carrying a tray with steaming cups of percolated coffee, not the usual instant stuff. Was this to impress me?

He sat down very close and we sipped. As soon as I'd put my cup down, he came even closer, and taking my hand in his rather pudgy one, he did **not** pledge undying love.

Instead he said "Clarice, I've always liked you, you turn me on, you know?"

I didn't speak, I was stunned into silence.

"How about you and me get together, nothing too sudden. I really like you and I'd like to know you better."

"What are you talking about, we're both married."

"But we've both been married for a long time and I fancy you. I have, since the first time I saw you."

"James, don't be ridiculous. It's out of the question."

"Why? Nobody would know. No-one gets hurt. It would be our little secret."

(Oh yes, I knew all about secrets, I'd had them before. The difference was, I'd never shared them with anyone else)

His hand was warm round mine. His leg was pressed hard against my thigh and I could see a slight swelling in his trousers. Perhaps they were just tight at the groin? I had never stared at his crutch before, though now I felt a magnetic pull to look again!

He put his arms round me and pulling me to him started kissing me, pushing his tongue deep inside my mouth. I made no effort to resist. Instead I melted. (What the hell was I doing?

Though, hadn't I known, deep down, that the garden invitation had been a quite unsubtle ploy)

We came up for breath and then he kissed me again. His tongue now at home in the deep recesses of my mouth and throat. Very sensual! I had never experienced anything like it.

"I'll take that as a 'Yes' then shall I?" James said.

That night I initiated sex with Terry. For reassurance that everything was OK and my life wasn't going to swing out of control again.

He was surprised as I was usually too tired in the week. It came to the usual satisfying climax, and I fell quickly into a deep sleep. Events of the day were temporarily erased.

A text appeared on my mobile! 'Tues @ noon?

The text I'd been both waiting for and dreading, finally arrived. It had seem like a month since I had sat in the garden, contemplating the Spring flowers!

He picked me up and took me home as before, chatting in the car about work and mundane things. Ginny, apparently never came home at lunchtime as she worked too far away. (I hoped fervently that she was never taken ill at lunch-time).

I didn't fancy yet another cup of coffee, as I'd had several at work in the morning, so he poured me some organic lemonade. I noticed the 'Telegraph', folded on the table, and asked if he did the crossword. If we bought a paper at home, we always got the 'Mail'!

"No," he said "Too boring" "So what **do** you like doing?" I continued. "I spend a lot of time reading, old books on cricket mostly. I collect them." Our conversation was so stilted, I knew this whole thing was a bad idea! I felt so nervous that a cold shiver ran through me. James noticed. "Are you cold Clarice?" he asked and came round from the other side of the table to put an arm round me, "Don't worry, I'll soon warm you up!"

This was becoming more and more like a second rate, black and white movie, than a meeting of two like minds! I began to think that I might giggle if the script got any more corny, but that thought was interrupted by James and his brand of kissing. I became wet through and felt any resistance I might have summoned, evaporate. My head had turned off and my body had taken over.

"Would you like to go somewhere more comfortable?" he asked between my gasps. I nodded and he led me to a downstairs bedroom, where one of his twins slept when he was home from Uni.

He left the room to lock the front door. Presumably, he'd also thought of the worst case scenario, that is of Ginny turning up unexpectedly.

I tore off all my clothes immediately, and leapt under the duvet, so ashamed was I of my body still, despite fighting those feelings all my life. It was as if I had suddenly allowed myself to be shamed, naked and humiliated. Under the duvet I lay shaking. I was too frozen to think.

James came in . "Clarice there was no need to strip off, I was going to undress you slowly "he said, "why did you do it?"

"I was a bit nervous" I muttered.

"But you're a married woman, there's nothing to be nervous about! Besides I've seen it all before. I saw you in that reality show, walking down the aisle covered only in ribbons! I've been wanting to fuck you ever since. Don't pretend to be shy!"

My wetness dried up like turning off a tap.

He got under the duvet with me. He had a very hairy chest and man-boobs. His stomach was fatter than I'd imagined. His well cut suits hid a lot.

He started the kissing which turned me back on to some extent. His fore play was limited to a quick, slightly painful pinch of each nipple and then some very lengthy cunnilingus, which began to bore me. He then penetrated me and did some nifty twisting movements deep inside, grunting a lot.

After quite a bit of perseverance, he came at last, panting and snorting, like a grampus. I did not climax, but obviously pretended to, as he was my boss.

I was shown to the downstairs bathroom, painted in raspberry pink, where I showered off his sweat.

He was ready in the kitchen with the coffee. I needed it now.

"Nice bathroom." I said, by way of conversation, "I love the raspberry colour, it's quite unusual for a bathroom."

"My wife's choice," he said, "I hate it. Not masculine enough for my taste."

Jo and I met for lunch the following Thursday, as arranged. She was glowing, as only happy, pregnant women can. I kept the conversation about her, and the forthcoming happy event as long as I could. It wasn't hard, she was brimming over with talk about relaxation classes, her birthing plan, whether to get a pram or a convertible push chair. I just listened and gave her the odd gem of advice, which I knew would not be taken, We ate pizza but she refused the parmisan cheese, She also ordered a side salad. Typical of Jo to behave in all the right ways. It took me back to when I has expecting Tom. I'd eaten bags and bags of chips drenched in tomato ketchup, washed down with Coke, and soared right up to thirteen and a half stone. Whereas Jo, now quite far on in the pregnancy, still looked quite trim apart from her bump.

Eventually she asked about me. How was Terry?...she'd never approved of him..

And little Tommy? Not so little now I thought

Finally, the dreaded question. Did I go to church in Debden?

"No Jo," I said, "I'm afraid I've lapsed a bit. You know how it is, working long hours. Can't ask Terry to look after Tom every Sunday, he works so hard."

I hammed it up a bit, because actually Tom was fairly self reliant and Terry was always happy to fit in with whatever I wanted to do. It was me. I made all sorts of excuses to myself, but basically I didn't want to go to church any more, it was part of another life. And how would I square it with my new one? The affair? I suppose that's what you'd call it, would be another hidden part of my life now. I knew it wouldn't be just a one off, because James had murmured in my ear before getting dressed.

"That **was** a surprise, but we haven't peaked yet!" I hadn't enjoyed the sex but the kissing was wonderful. If I was honest, the danger factor also turned me on. A wicked secret that I shared with the big boss-man!

What was the eleventh commandment? Ah yes, 'Thou shalt not be caught'

Jo pretended to understand about my commitments, my genuine ones, anyway. She'd have had an attack of the vapours if she ever found out about James! But it was obviously hard for her to put herself in my shoes. She shared the Christian ethos with her husband. The Church was their whole way of life, and their little one would be brought up in the faith. I was ashamed to say I'd never even thought of sending Tom to Sunday school. It had all sounded a bit old fashioned.

There were times though, that I'd remembered the friends at the Club, and singing in the little choir. I also knew that the Frinton weekend had pulled me from the depths of despair. But that was partly it! I didn't want to remember too much of what I had been, in case it pulled me back to what I was then. Deep down I knew that the real me hadn't changed. I was still struggling not to drown.

We parted as friends do, with a hug and a promise to meet again soon. I knew that wouldn't happen, but I would send her a present for the new arrival when the baby's card announcing the baby's birth came in the post. I wished her "Good luck for the labour, if I don't see you before!" and we went our separate ways.

James and I met for what he called our 'assignations' and I called 'extended coffee' breaks, weekly or fortnightly for months. I was always at his disposal. I got quite fond of him in a romantic story book sort of way, though despite every sexual position known to man, with oral sex, ad nauseam (and I mean till I was nearly sick one time) he **never** delivered. I was undoubtedly flattered by the attention of the now Senior Partner. Why pick me? Despite what everyone always said to the contrary, I knew what a shapeless, ugly body I had. James continued to make a lot of comments, though we never had a proper conversation, because we actually had nothing in common. He said that I was sweet natured. that there was chemistry between us. He said that even if he didn't see me for weeks, it didn't mean it was over between us. He pronounced that 'all women ever wanted was love and all men ever wanted was sex.'(which might be true of a lot of women, but didn't apply to me.) He bought me a blue vibrator. I must have mentioned to him that blue was my favourite colour, but to me it looked decidedly cyanosed, though the tortuous plastic veins looked strangely familiar! I threw it in the bin on the way home, partly because Terry would know that I would never have dared go into an Ann Summers shop to make a purchase, and partly because I didn't need mechanical aids to orgasm, while Terry was around. James never bought me flowers again, and even more sadly, no chocolates!

Christmas came round again quickly, I simply couldn't believe how the months had flown, and this time, work seemed busier than ever. The patients poured in for flu jabs and then the ones who hadn't bothered to take up the offer of inmmunisation, got ill and called for home visits **for** the flu. The typing fell off a bit, so I was drafted in to help in Reception, as people forgot about insurances in favour of Christmas shopping and works parties.

The Season of Good will .

The weather was so grim. Piles of early snow heaped up in the gutters, icicles hanging from trees, the roads, sheet ice. It would have looked pretty on a Christmas card stamped with a large red-breasted robin, but for pedestrians and drivers alike, it was treacherous.

Our trio were so worn out on the last Friday before the holiday that we could hardly drag ourselves to the pub. The fire was raging and the Landlord beamed as we took up our usual seats.

Before we could speak we each downed a glass of red wine. The barman brought us over a plate of sandwiches with olives and pickled onions and we were all set for our usual hilarious de-briefing.

Nic started "Well, I wouldn't like to have another week like that in a hurry! Why do all those old codgers leave it to the last minute to ask for their repeats?"

"God only knows!" said Lara, "I'm sick to death of the whole thing. After Christmas I'm going to look for another job."

"Really!" Nic and I chorused, we laughed and intertwined our little fingers and shook them, as a sign of good luck. She continued "Don't Lara, don't leave us. We'll miss you terribly, won't we Clarice?"

"Have you thought what else to do?" I asked, "There's not much going on round this area. I looked round for ages before I got this job. I s'pose things might have taken off a bit now though." I added

"Thanks for the thought! Great to have good mates like you." She said "but I thought of moving up to Epping to be near my new boy friend, there's quite a bit going on there. I might get a job in a shop or something like that."

"Tell you what I fancy "said Nicole, "working in a sports centre, like 'David Lloyds.' You'd see healthy people there and some fit men!"

"I thought you were happy with Mark "I said

"Yes I am, but a girl likes to look around. I wouldn't **do** anything, it would just be eye-candy."

"Well I never thought of you in that light, Nic. I thought you were all wholesome and sporty." I said

"Sports people are the worst" she said "All that running and jumping gets their endorphins going. And other things!" she giggled .

The second bottle of wine was nearly gone, but the night was still young. I'd really had enough booze after a tiring day but the others kept on knocking it back. I noticed Nicole was slowing down a bit.

"What's your new man called?" Lara I asked

"Keith" she said "but he's not much cop. I've known him since I was at school. He's got Narcolepsy, so he keeps going to sleep on the job!"

I looked at her to see if she was joking.

"No, really" she said, He's not well. He needs a carer more than a girl friend, but he is decent"

"What about another bottle?" asked Lara, I want to get smashed tonight."

NIc stood up "I'm going to go to the loo. I think I've had enough. Does anyone want some water?"

"Yes, that's a good idea." I said "Could you get me some too?"

"I'll get a jug and a couple of glasses."

Lara drank most of the next bottle on her own and to my dismay asked the barman to bring another. She wasn't slurring her words, but she was talking rather loudly and starting to gesticulate.

"Keith's alright, not like that other ponce!" "D'ya mean Doug?" I asked

"No, Not Doug, Doug's ok, we just fell out!"

"Who do you mean, Lara? Anyone we know?" I probed

"Yer, You know him all right. That sleazebag, James."

"What d'you mean Lara?" I asked

"The great Dr Thorpe with his dirty little dick! Used to pick me up in his shagging wagon with the tinted windows and do it there and then, if he couldn't wait!" She took a few more gulps of wine.

"Always rushing! The times he's had me on the downstairs bed, always quick, in case his wife showed up." Her speech became garbled. I couldn't speak. Surely not my James!

Lara continued "All those showers in that shitty, pink bathroom."

"We need to get her home now," I said to Nic. We all piled into the cab when it arrived. Lara in the front. Before I was dropped off, I paid Lara's fare as well as my own, and prayed she wouldn't vomit in the taxi."

It obsessed me all over the Christmas weekend. Through dressing the tree and watching Trevor stuff the turkey. Through Tom's excitement at opening his presents! During the Queens speech, I thought of him doing it to her, a girl half his age. Plump and spotty, but no doubt, easy meat!

Back at work, I waited a week to discuss it with Nicole, while she skied in France.

"What do you think Nic, did James really sleep with Lara, What do you think the truth of the matter is?"

"Well," she said "I talked about it to my husband and daughter, and they said knowing Lara, they thought she must have made it up. I mean it's a bit unlikely, isn't it. The senior partner with our Lara. We decided she must have been fantasising about him, and all that drink had made her believe it was true. I mean she was absolutely plastered, wasn't she?" I frowned

"Maybe you're right," I said, but the give away for me had been when she mentioned the pink bathroom. The only other possibility was that she had seen that bathroom at one of the BBQs held at James's house before I joined the practice, and it had stuck in her mind. It was a very unusual colour. Could she have woven a 'wannabe' situation around her infatuation for the boss. It had been done before.

I rang him at home that lunch-time. The first time I'd ever risked contacting him like that. When he answered, probably thinking it was the surgery letting him know he had a new home visit, he sounded startled to hear my voice!

"Clarice?" he asked "How can I help you?"

"James I want to ask you something," by my tone he could tell I was annoyed.

"Hang on a minute. I've got my son here. I can't talk now. I'll ring you back."

'Son?' I thought 'or yet another woman?'

By the time he rang back I was fuming and shaking. I came straight to the point.

"Have you had an affair with Lara? She says you have!"

"There is truth in it."

"What do you mean there's truth it? Either you have or you haven't!"

"Well look, I should have told you. She really gets on my nerves that girl, I've been wanting to sack her, but I haven't got the grounds yet."

"What do you mean? Have you, or have you not had an affair with Lara?"

"She threw herself at me. How could I refuse, she's less than half my age. It was too good an offer to turn down!"

"You disgust me. She's had such a hard upbringing! How **could** you, Someone she should have been able to look up to. You must have groomed her." He was silent. "And what about Gina? Is that why she left so suddenly? Did you have a go at her too?"

"Look" he said "It's a free country . Gina was quite willing in the beginning. I never said I was perfect."

"No, but you didn't tell me you were a predator, going after young girls. A serial adulterer! Does Ginny know about all this?"

His voice changed from arrogant to slightly shaky "No and she must never know."

And then he had the sheer grossness to add,"It needn't change anything between us you know." I hang up and went to be sick.

Chapter 9

Guilt is a two edged sword.

On James's side of the blade, he felt none.

On mine, the sharpness of what I'd done to Terry, cut me deeply.

I was also angry at being used...very! I felt stupid and annoyed. I felt none of it had been the slightest bit worthwhile. I was disgusted with myself, but more, I felt furious that much younger girls than me, had also been his prey. And one of those, Gina, had been too upset to stay in her job.

Ginny was another whole topic. Did she really not know what her husband had been up to. Maybe there were many more women out there who had just been notches on his cane.

My fragile self image had been severely battered, but what about Lara? She was fast becoming an alcoholic.

I knew there was nothing I could do. To expose him would lay my self open to blame, and destroy my marriage. Ginny would also get hurt in the slipstream.

All I could do now was support Lara, indirectly, and lie low, myself.

How flattery can make fools of us all!

January passed uneventfully. James didn't come for coffee in the typing room any more, he put his work in my in-tray, like the other partners. He stayed away, avoiding me whenever he could. Instead, he struck up conversations with other members of the staff.

It wasn't long before I realised that he must have diverted his attention to yet another helpless target, and started the grooming process all over again. I hoped it was someone away from Willow Green.

Lara had another 'heart to heart' with me in the common room one Friday. We drank tea now. The Friday nights had stopped, by silent, but common consent. After the pre-Christmas revelations, none of us had the stomach for further boozy sessions.

"Clarice, can I have a word?" Lara began.

"Yes of course, what's it about?"

"It's my drinking" she said, "I don't just drink at party times any more I've started drinking every night, at home. Mum doesn't know what to do. If she says anything I go mad at her. But I know I've totally lost control."

"What about your new boy-friend, Lara? What does he say? Can he help you?" I asked

"No, there is no boyfriend. He couldn't stand me always being drunk round him, anymore than Mum can."

"Lara there are lots of people that can help you." I said "I gave a list out to one of the patients, only last week. There's AA, or maybe you should get some individual therapy. Have you been to your GP?"

She burst into tears, smudging her mascara, as she tried to wipe her eyes.

"Look, go to one of the partners here, Felicity's kind and quite approachable, if you're afraid to go to your own GP. I'm sure she wouldn't mind, or there's a drop-in centre in Ilford, I saw it on the list. You could get your mum to give you a lift over."

"Thanks, Clarice, she said, drying her eyes on some paper towel, "You're a real mate. I'll think about it." She went back to her desk in Reception.

I felt a schmuck. Too many emotions, tripping over each other for me to think clearly!

Late that night, Terry asked if I was alright. "You haven't been acting quite yourself recently. What's up, pet?"

"I'm thinking of changing my job" I said.

Baby Meg was so sweet. I took her a smocked dress for her to wear in the Spring, when she was bigger.

Jo was thrilled to see me!

I asked her all about the birth. Had it been too long or painful ?

No, She'd had a water-birth and Meg had just slipped out.

"Funny that," I said "I'd always thought the baby might drown in the water."

She laughed "No, silly it's not started using its lungs before birth. It's been swimming around in the amniotic fluid inside. It just changes one fluid for another. When Meg was born they lifted her out like a mermaid, Rod cut the cord and she started to gulp in air and cried straight away!"

"I grinned "Oh, what an idiot! Of course, I never thought of that."

"Thanks for the dress Clarice it's beautiful. Is it hand smocked?" Jo asked

"Yes, I think so, but I'm afraid I didn't do it. No time, and I never learnt how to sew, more's the pity!"

"So, Clarice, how have you been since we last met."

"I'm looking for another job." I said

"But I thought you were really happy at the Health Centre? Is everything OK?

How's Terry?"

"Yes, we're all fine." I replied "But, you know, I'm getting itchy feet. Never was one to hang around in one place for long."

"That's true." She said "I'm more of a stick in the mud. A conservative with a small 'c', I suppose. How are your Mum and Dad. I never did get to meet them." Said Jo

"Mum's alright, but Dad's in the later stages of Dementia."

"Oh, I am sorry. Do you have to go up and help out much? Give her a bit of support?"

"No, I haven't had time lately. And I don't drive." 'More guilt!' I thought. "She's got Prue and Trevor's grown into a strong lad. Her sister, Joyce, lives just down the road. But I will be popping up soon." I added.

"We're having a Dedication Service for Meg in a couple of months. We would love you to come. Maybe you could become a 'Prayer partner' for her as well, seeing as you and I were so close?"

"Thanks Jo" I said "I'll look forward to the invitation"

Waiting at the bus stop my mind staggered. 'The dedication', a 'prayer partner' Had Jo and I really been that close?

If she knew what I'd become! An uncaring, vain, and deceitful adulterer! If she did know, I would immediately plummet to the bottom of her list of Meg's prospective 'Prayer partners'.

I passed a cake shop on the way from the bus and bought a dozen cream éclairs.

By the time Terry got home, picking up Tom on the way home, from his friend's house, I'd eaten and regurgitated the lot!

"What's for supper" called Tom as he came through the front door.

The sun came out and shone brightly in March, because our syndicate had a Lottery win! Unbelievable! So we hadn't just been rolling our £1 coins down the drain, after all.

Not a life-changing amount, but we worked out each of us eight girls in the Syndicate would receive £750,000!

Terry was over the moon! He'd spent it about three times over before he calmed down. "Family first." Though, he said. Terry had a widowed father he hadn't seen for years, but he should definitely get some help from us. He'd never asked any thing from his son all his life, and we weren't even sure if he still lived at the same address, or even if he was still alive!

Terry agreed that my Mum ought to have a tidy sum, to help her with Dad's care; and we then would put some into savings in trust for Tom, for when he was older.

The rest was ours. To assuage my guilt, I let Terry decide what we should do with the rest of the money. I knew, in any case, he would always think of my needs first. That was his nature.

I gave my notice in the following week. They were going to be a bit short staffed for the time being as Nicole and Lara had already handed theirs in.

Terry looked into some investment options, to give us security in the long term, and took out life insurance for each of us, to protect our darling only son, in the long term. We were both fit as fiddles. Well Terry was, anyway. He spent every day running up and down scaffolding, when he wasn't loading up lorries or driving fork lift trucks. His job description had changed quite a bit since I'd first met him. Then, he used to be a craftsman carpenter, making furniture to order, nowadays all that stuff was made en masse in the factories and Terry had moved in to construction work. In some ways he missed the fiddling about with wood, but he had got used to the more active life, and said he preferred charging round the building sites, to staying inside all the time. Last year, they had made him a foreman. At home, the garden fulfilled his creative urges.

After all the serious stuff, Terry announced that the three of us were going on a foreign holiday.

"Some place where the sun always shines!" he told us one evening.

The following Saturday, Terry took Tom down to 'Bath Travel' in Loughton and they both came back loaded down with holiday brochures.

Terry was the most excited I have ever seen him.

The three of us talked of nothing else but the proposed holiday.

Tom fancied the thrill of camel rides to see the Pyramids and the Sphynx in Egypt.

I liked the sound of the mystical Maldives, where some of the islands were barely able to rise above the turquoise ocean. I'd seen it on travel programs and now the brochure said its sunsets were out of this world.

I wasn't so keen on the small print which said as the islands were Moslem, topless bathing could land you up in prison. Not a nice end to a perfect holiday!

Terry didn't mind where we went. He was like a dog with an extremely juicy bone!

"If we can't all agree, we'll take it in turns to choose, and go somewhere different every holiday. We can afford it now, thanks to Mum" He smiled at me lovingly.

He touched my arm, "The world's our oyster now, isn't it, pet" he asked.

"Think of all the planning! Do you think they'd let us take Tom out of school? It would be less crowded in the term. We could say travel was part of his education!" he laughed

"That was about the longest speech I've ever heard you make." I said to him

"Well I'm so happy, Clarice! It makes me garrulous, if that's the right word?"

"Anyway," he gabbled on, "I want to go to an island far, far away, and dream I'm in Paradise with you," He squeezed my arm .

"Hey, what about me?" Tom chipped in

"Oh and you of course, we wouldn't go anywhere without you!"

I took a breath for him. I realised I had never given Terry much of my thinking space. Where did his mind wander while he hammered away, in his early days as a chippy? Had he always had an imaginative life that I had never known about? Had he been musing on all sorts of possibilities, while the macho men around him weren't? What did he think about? Had he always dreamed about journeying to exotic islands? What other hopes and dreams did he have that I had never bothered to ask him about?

Had I been so self obsessed that I had never noticed his more tender feelings?

"What about Barbados then?" I asked suddenly. "That sounds like a dream island."

We talked long into the night. I was worried that Tom wouldn't be able to get up for school in the morning. He seemed to need lots of sleep now he was growing so fast. His arms and legs seemed to be extending out of his shirt sleeves and trouser legs like a sprouting bean pole. Never mind, I hadn't the heart to break up the happy party by sending him to bed. Both my T's were talking at the same time, hardly listening to each other. Tom was saying about the camels and Pyramids again "We've been doing it at school." He finished. "Tom listen," said his Dad, "I've told you we can go there next time." "What this summer holidays, if we go to Barbados in the Spring?" Tom was determined to get his way if he could

"We'll see," said Terry. "Actually, it might be a bit too hot in Egypt in August."

During the following week, I began to have collywobbles about the trip. Why wasn't I as excited about it as the boys? I did fancy a big holiday, somewhere warm. I tried to think what was worrying me. I had never been out of the country before, but more than that I had never flown. Suddenly the thought of flying overwhelmed me. Could I manage a short flight? Was it just the long haul that worried me? No I suddenly realised I would be frightened to death of flying! I didn't want to put a damper on things. What should I say?

On the next Saturday night, the boys had all the holiday brochures out again on the dining room table, and were poring over them.

I had to say something.

"I know we said Barbados, but it is a long way away. What about the Continent? We haven't even considered Spain or Italy. Italy's got some amazing ancient sites too Tom. What about Pompeii where all those people got turned to stone when the lava covered them. We could go to Capri and be rowed into the Blue Grotto." It was my turn to ramble "Or France, we could go up the Eiffel Tower. That would be exciting!"

"Muumm!" We could go there any time. They might do a trip like that from school. It's much too ordinary! We'd probably go on Eurostar, anyway if we go from school."

"Exactly my point,Tom." I said "We could go by Eurostar ourselves and then coach and more trains, all over Europe, if you like!"

Terry looked up from the brochure that he was engrossed in.

"Clarice what are you trying to say, pet? I think I know where this is coming from. Are you scared of flying?"

I had to admit I was!

Terry thought for a moment.

"I know," he said "we'll get you hypnotised. I've heard it works for 'Flying Phobia.' In fact Ron's wife Jackie went to a hypnotist before they went to Majorca last year. Their GP refused to give her Valium for the trip and she was terrified. But after one session with the hypnotist she was fine. I'll get all the details from Ron on Monday, if you like." He smiled and squeezed my hand "Don't worry darling." He said.

He had never called me that before! In all our married life, I realised that I had never truly valued him, yet his love for me shone out of his smile. He would do anything for me. Why hadn't I been more caring and considerate all those years?

"Ok, I'll give it a go, if you think it'll work."

On the door was a silver plate engraved with the words 'Dr Ernest Baverstock M.D. Dip. Hyp. N.L.P. Practitioner'

I rang the bell. An elderly man came to the door looking as if he had just walked out of a Sherlock Holmes' movie. He had a pointed, 'salt and pepper' coloured beard and deep set grey eyes behind thick glasses. He wore a tweed jacket and tan waist coat, but didn't sport plus-fours (Thank goodness!) In fact he looked exactly how I would have expected a hypnotist to look, so I was half way cured already!

""Dr Baverstock" he said by way of introduction, and bowed slightly,

I took his outstretched hand and said "How do you do, I'm Clarice."

"Well I'm very pleased to meet you, Clarice. You said on the phone that you needed to feel more confident while you were sitting in an aeroplane." I noticed that he didn't actually mention the word 'Flying'!

"Yes" I said, but omitted to say that I was scared shitless!

"Do take a seat, my dear." He paused while I sat comfortably

"As I said on the telephone, throughout this trance you will always remain completely in control. The only side effects of hypnosis is an increased feeling of well-being." I nodded.

He started. "I would like you to imagine you are standing on a balcony… and there is a long flight of stairs leading down from this balcony… In a few seconds I am going to count from 10 to 1 and…you are going to feel more… and more…relaxed with each descending number…and with each descending number… you will take a single step down… and feel more and more relaxed…" He murmured on and I started to feel strangely calm,…" going into a wonderful place," I heard him say "a place of complete relaxation"

The next thing I remember was Dr Baverstock counting "8…9…10… Wake up now, Wide awake! Have a good stretch!"

I paid and left his rooms, still in a slight daze, thinking that the street looked exceedingly bright.

Terry was waiting in the car, outside.

"How did it go?" he asked.

"Give me a minute," I said.

Well, the hypnosis must have worked miracles, because by the next weekend we had agreed on Barbados as our definite holiday destination.

There was no more argument. The brochure said, 'Barbados is a small but beautiful island with stunning beaches, friendly people and a serene atmosphere.' Wow, hot sunny days and rum punches (fruit ones for Tom of course). Hopping to other Carribean islands, Barbecues on the beach in the evening to the sound of Calypso. We all chipped in and helped to draw the picture.

Terry booked it for the school's Easter holidays. We couldn't decide, one week or two, but in the end Tom persuaded Terry to settle for the eighteen day break, as he had a lot of holiday owing him from work.

At last, my dream life was coming true, and even better it seemed that Terry shared that dream.

I didn't even have to ask for time off work now that I'd left the Health Centre.

Sod James and sod the whole lot of them, Terry and I were going to have a ball. First of all, we would share the dream with Tom and then, later, when he had taken off for a life of his own, we'd just have each other. Then we could have a proper honeymoon, just the two of us. The honeymoon we had never been able to have when we got married.

I'd make it up to Terry. I was even more loving than usual. I would put all that awful business with James behind me. It would be as nothing, I wouldn't even remember it, and the best of it was, Terry would never know.

Our passports came through about six weeks before we were due to leave. We all had a good laugh at the photos and wondered why they had insisted we remained totally poker-faced for the mug shots? Did a smile really make us unrecognisable?

Now we had to go and buy ourselves some new clothes for the holiday. I took Tom to M&S to set him up with new jeans and a couple of T-shirts 'goodness knows if they'll fit him by then, the way he's growing' I thought; and some of those long droopy bathing trunks that boys insisted wearing . Speedo's were only worn by Olympic swimmers these days.

I bought myself a pale blue sundress, and a white bikini that I knew Terry would approve of. I wasn't worried if I'd get too fat for it before the holiday. I'd known for years how to stay at the same weight, whatever I ate.

Sunglasses and high factor sun cream were ticked off the list.

Money, we could get at the airport and anything else we forgot we could buy in Barbados. Hurray!!

We were going from Heathrow to the Hotel Paradiso!

Should we take the car to the airport or book a taxi? I thought Terry might be too tired after the long trip back, so we booked a cab, each way.

Years ago Terry might have argued about cabs being a waste of money, but now he agreed that my idea was a very good one. These days we always agreed about pretty much everything. I realised that Terry was the love of my life and despite my lapse, always had been!

Chapter 10

The days till our holiday were flying by.

I thought that stopping working, would make my days would seem a bit empty, so I had thought up some ideas for filling them. I could meet Jo for coffee, though I realised that she might be too busy with little Meg? I could swan up to London to visit Harrods, and at least buy one of their carrier bags. That's what people did, I'd heard, to show off that they had been customers of the pricey store. In fact, since the Lottery win, I could actually buy almost anything I wanted at Harrods. Maybe I should join the Gym and do some work outs, to get 'the body beautiful', before our holiday. I could even get some tanning sessions, so that the Barbados's sun didn't make me all red on the first day. If all else failed, I might go and watch a film with subtitles, at the local Arts cinema, isn't that what rich people do, or do you have to be brainy as well, to understand the films' deep meaning? Now we had money, I felt I needed to improve my standing in society and embrace 'Culture' whatever that was. Do the things that rich and clever people did. I knew there would always be a gulf between my beginnings and now. I had never become Kathy's replica, no matter how hard I'd tried. Had Terry held me back? Socially, I mean. I hated myself for even giving that thought daylight. He was the best and dearest thing that had ever happened to me. If he did have a bad side somewhere, hidden away, and we all live with the 'Shadow', he had certainly always kept it out of my sight. I was the ugly one, on the inside at least.

All these ruminations did me no good. I knew deep down what I should do. And that was, visit my Mother. Give her some time, now I had no more excuses about work keeping me too busy.

Somehow, I couldn't bear to go and find out how bad things had become at home. I dreaded seeing my father's deterioration for myself, though Trevor had rung me to say things were getting pretty bad. Since the time of our Christmas visit, I had kept in touch, but only by phone. Trevor had now become my Dad's full-time carer, and drew the statutory carer's benefit. It wasn't much. My mother helped him, of course, but she wasn't strong enough to lift Dad on her own. They were chronically short of money, so my Mum went out and did a little cleaning job.

They wouldn't take any of the money we offered them, so instead we tried to buy them things they needed. But I knew, in my heart of hearts, that what they really wanted, was for me to visit. It would do them more good than any amount of money or things I could send.

I couldn't drive of course, but then, in the past, I'd always gone by train. It was true that Tom needed me, but not that much. Terry ought to come home to a proper cooked supper after a long day at work. What rubbish all these excuses were!

The fact was I couldn't face it. Memories of my childhood swept though my mind, ominously, like dark clouds in a previously clear blue sky. Memories of Dad's tempers. His drinking. Mum's pandering to my twee little sister, always having allowances made for her, because she was thin and eat like a bird. Getting the best of everything, which in our family wasn't much, because Dad drank the money away. Then, there was poor little Trev with his missing fingers. Now he was going to miss out again. Miss out on life, while caring for the parent who had despised him throughout his childhood. My poor family, what a mess our home life had been, and I was the only one who had managed to escape. I tried to fight off the guilty feelings that always hovered near to the surface.

A couple of weeks before our holiday, I decided to go and visit Jo. Maybe I could tell her a bit about my childhood. How it still hurt. About my guilty conscience over Mum.

Jo was my only true friend. That was my fault. I made friends easily, but when I moved on, I dropped them.

Staying in contact with people was hard for me.

I'd lost touch with Kathy and never bothered to find out how her children were, or how they were shaping up as they grew older. They must be quite big now, dear little Jamie and Lois. I tried to work out their ages. They must, at least be teenagers. Was she still with Dave? I wondered, but I had left it all too late to enquire. The last contact had been when she had given me a reference for the Heath centre post.

The salon girls had been fun, but at the time I'd been distracted with Tommy, and we'd been looking for a bigger place to live.

I had tried to put the memories of 'Willow Green' out of my mind, for obvious reasons. My shameful behaviour during my last year there had been, more or less successfully, placed under lock and key, in a sealed compartment of my mind. Hopefully, the knowledge of what I had done would die with me! I often wondered what had happened to Lara, though. I had no contact number for her. The last thing I'd heard, she had moved from her mum's and was working at a hospital in London.

Jo was thrilled to see me! "Hi Clarice, I'm so glad you could come over. Meg can nearly sit up now!"

We went through into the kitchen and there in the corner, surrounded by cushions propping her up, was dear little Meg.

"Hello Meg," I said getting down to her level, and sitting on the floor beside her. She was shaking her rattle at me, with glee. I took this as a welcoming sign, since she couldn't speak yet! She had pink cheeks and was very smiley, looking, to me, exactly like a picture of a cherubic tiny tot in the 'Mabel Lucie Attwell's annual I'd had at home when I was a child.

"What a lovely baby, Jo!" I said. "People say all babies are lovely, But she is delicious! Those eyes and those little chubby cheeks! It makes me want to smile just to look at her!"

Jo grinned "Thanks, Clarice. We think the sun shines out of her. Rod is besotted!"

I was so glad that I'd decided to go round to Jo's. I had felt a bit nervous. I knew that the fact that I hadn't turned out to be the Christian she'd tried so hard to make me, had disappointed her. But somehow a baby heals all those kinds of divisions.

We had lunch, scrambled egg on toast with tomatoes. Meg sat in her high chair and was fed some sort of mush with a spoon, before having her bottle.

After winding and nappy changing, all the other things I'd forgotten you had to do when you had a baby, Meg laid her gently in her cot for her afternoon nap.

We went back to the kitchen to wash up and Jo put the kettle on for a cup of tea.

We sat down to drink it. I could see Jo was tired from all the broken nights she'd being having. Getting Meg back to sleep, soothing her colic, making up her feeds and all the other work, that babies, however sweet, engender. I wondered if I was right to burden her with all the problems around my upbringing. It seemed unfair of me to put even the slightest dampener on this picture of total domestic happiness.

I pulled out the poof, for Jo to put her feet on, so that she could rest her legs while Meg was napping. As I was doing this, and emphasising that Jo must always make the most of any her free time she could grab while the baby slept, my mobile rang.

That's funny, I thought, as I picked it up, no one ever calls me in the day! If Terry rings me at all, it's either to let me know he's going to be late home from work, or asking if I mind him popping round to Ron's on the way home for a beer.

Was I Clarice, the voice asked? Mrs Clarice Smith? That's strange, I thought, nobody ever uses my surname.

"It's the police here. I'm afraid there's been an accident."

Then began my 'dark night' of the soul.

From the moment I heard that Terry was dead, till the time of his funeral, my brain was suffused with pain. Nothing was blanked out, but nothing made sense to me any more.

Instead, my mind, spinning with shards of disconnected thoughts, was sent into free fall. Confusion reigned.

I couldn't make sense of anything they tried to tell me.

They said he had been hit by a crane shifting concrete blocks.

"He didn't suffer,"

"It was instant."

"His hard hat couldn't save him."

I was deluged by a stream of meaningless information from police and hospital. People I'd never heard of, sent their condolences.

The funeral was going to be delayed because of investigation about the cause of the accident.

I decided to send Tom up to my Mum's. Trevor came down to collect him, and it was agreed that they would keep him till the funeral.

I wasn't interested in the whys and wherefores of how the accident had been allowed to happen, how to apportion blame, or what compensation I would receive. All I knew was Terry was dead. Life as I knew it was over. I was dead inside.

Ron helped me make the arrangements for the funeral, when at last the body was released.

I decided on a cremation. I couldn't bear the thought of the warm man who had shared my bed, lying alone in the cold, unyielding earth. Much better that he should become a puff of smoke and fly free to join the angels.

I couldn't think about order of service, so Ron came with me to ask the Crematorium's resident vicar if he would take over the proceedings.

I chose 'All things bright and beautiful' as it was the only hymn I could remember, and thought vaguely that even the most hardened atheist would know the tune. But who would come? Were people invited to a funeral? Or did they just turn up? I had no idea. As it was, Mum couldn't come down because Dad's carer phoned in sick on the day. Tom was brought down by Trevor, with Prue and the boyfriend. I remember thinking how well Phil had scrubbed up.

Tom looked very pale with red-rimmed eyes, wearing his slightly too-short school trousers. How different he would have looked in the Barbadian sunshine.

Prue cried throughout the service, though she hardly knew Terry. This whole occasion was the first brush she'd had with death, and coming to terms with her own fragile mortality, racked her with sobs.

The coffin bearing my husband, now and forever quite alone, lay on the plinth.

As Rod Stewart's 'Sailing' started to play through the loud speakers, the coffin began to glide smoothly towards the furnace. Gradually, the thick velvet curtains swept round it, and my darling Terry was consigned to a place at least as hot as Hell…if Hell existed.

It was terrifying. I tried to think 'it's only his earthly remains'. But what else had I held every night? Who else had I talked to, planned a holiday of a life time with? What had I known about Terry, except his earthly remains?

The only thing we can know about anyone is what we can perceive with our five senses. Otherwise they wouldn't exist for us.

Only a few days before I had seen Terry, or rather, viewed his embalmed body lying in the blue satin-lined coffin, nothing cheap or throw-away for him. Not since the big win, the win that was going to change our lives completely.

But now, it wasn't going to be the metamorphosis into the life of social butterflies for which we had hoped, instead my life changed into the existence of a death moth.

Afterwards came 'the Wake'. What a strange name for a rite that marks the final sleep of the main player.

The next day, I sent Tom up to stay with Mum as long as she could have him, and I went into a state of suspended animation.

I was numb and useless. Just as Terry had been my rock in life, so Jo became my strength and stay after his death.

She helped me open and read a mass of cards and letters from people I hardly knew. They all contained similar sounding platitudes.

'I can/cannot imagine how awful you are feeling'
'What a terrible shock, you poor thing!' etc
And the inevitable 'Time will heal.'
There were even some unexpectedly religious ones
'The Lord is my shepherd.' And 'He is resting in the arms of Jesus.'
Jo dealt with them all.

Jo rang me every morning, but if she wasn't able to see me during the day, mild panic set in. Jumbled memories would swill through my mind. I could not think straight. Guilt and sadness mingled into a tangle of grief. I felt so guilty, about everything, but especially the affair. How could I have done that to Terry? Supposing Tom had found out that I'd betrayed his father?
Everything reminded me of Terry.
The tickets for our holiday came through. I'd forgotten to cancel them.
I thought of how we would have been, all together on holiday.' A holiday of a life time!' That hackneyed phrase. But it would have been true for us. And now we had no life time left to

enjoy. It had been eaten up by death. I remembered that lovely Sunday when Terry had helped build a complicated system of canals in the sand, with Tom. The memory of them laughing and joking together made me tremble. Then for the first time since Terry's accident, the accident, that had ended our lives together, I broke down and wept. The sobbing wrenched my heart. It shook me through and through, until I ended up exhausted with no more strength, my head throbbing and snot running down from my nose.

Guilt overwhelmed me.

I had been so callous about my own mother's suffering. I had never given her any moral support. Never even phoned to see how she was, all those years that she had been watching her own husband, my father, die a slow death, from a disease, so terrible, that it took away every vestige of the sufferer's self respect. I cried again at my own selfishness.

And then I looked out at the hanging baskets waiting to be filled, baskets that would never bloom again, and I lost it completely.

Jo tried her best to comfort me, but I became unable to make the simplest decision.

When she and Rod came round to talk to me about Tom, that evening, it was decided to try to get him into the Comprehensive, in Chester, near my Mum's, till I felt better able to cope.

Rod worked in Education and contacted the head of 'Kingsley Middle school'

Thanks to him it was all sorted, and Tom was to stay up there and join the same school Trevor had attended. The arrangement was for just one term, to begin with to give me a chance to pull my life back together again, and be able to give Tom a proper home again.

One morning, soon after Tom had gone to my Mum's, a strange, but rather wonderful thing happened. Nights hadn't been easy for me, since Terry's death. I managed to get off to sleep alright, but woke in the early hours of the morning cold and shivering, missing his warmth beside me, always forgetting that that warmth had gone forever. This particular morning, I opened my eyes slowly and slightly painfully, as they were sore and swollen from crying the previous night. Early sun rays streamed in through the half drawn bedroom curtains and there in the dark green wicker chair, in the corner of the room sat Terry.

He was smiling sweetly at me, saying 'Hello pet, how are you doing?' His clothes were pale and they had a flimsy, almost crystalline look to them... He said 'I've been watching you and you're doing all right.' He smiled again. I was speechless, but quickly slid out of bed to rush over and hug him, but just as I nearly reached up to him, he just melted away before my eyes, leaving an empty chair.

I went to make a strong cup of coffee. If only Tom had been there to see him. As soon as 9 o'clock came, knowing Rod would have left for work, I phoned Jo.

She picked up the phone and said "Hello?" in a rather bleary voice, wondering who on earth could be calling at this time in the morning. I guessed she been up in the night with Meg

"Jo, guess what?" I said "He came back. Terry came back to see me!"

"I'll come round ," she said "As soon as I given Meg her breakfast."

I was elated! I danced around, laughing in the shower. I didn't even stop to question the apparition. 'He **is** still here' I thought 'He is with me. He'll never leave me.'

As soon as Jo arrived she hugged me and said she was so glad I had cheered up. I told her again what had happened, that Terry actually been in our bedroom, sitting in the wicker chair!

"Well Clarice," she said, "I've heard of this sort of thing happening before, I can see it's made you feel a lot better."

To her credit, particularly being a Christian, she didn't say I'd imagined it. She didn't say that it was a projection of my distraught mind. Nor did she say that only unbelievers, who aren't accepted into heaven, hang around because their souls have no resting place, striving to be back where they belonged before death. She was simply kind and supportive.

"I've heard a lot of bereaved people do see their loved ones again." She reiterated. "It helps them through the grieving process."

Well, it certainly helped me. I hugged Jo with the baby still in her arms, and a few tears, now of relief, slid down my cheeks.

After that, Terry visited me a few more times, always in the early morning and always sitting in the same chair. As the weeks went by, although he always smiled at me, he became more and more translucent, until one morning I could hardly discern him at all, and then he simply faded away.

With Jo's persuasion I went back to the Church with her and Rod. Meg was put in the church's crèche: Only on Sunday mornings though, as I found it impossible to leave home in the evening. Jo hoped I'd join the choir again as she knew that was the bit of the service that I had really enjoyed, but with Terry gone, I knew I'd never sing again!

Members of the congregation were very kind and welcoming, saying they were so sorry to hear of my loss, but never appearing to pity me, which was kind.

Gradually I became more and more reclusive, though. I could hardly bear to go out. I wanted to stay in our home where I felt Terry's spirit was. If he tried to show himself again, I wanted to be there.

At first, I couldn't go shopping, and started having it brought to the door by the Tesco home delivery service. Soon, I couldn't even go to the church, with Jo and Rod, even though they had always offered to pick me up in their car.

Jo was worried.

"Look Clarice" she said "I know how upset you are over Terry, but you can't just hide in your house all the time. He would be worried too if he knew how unhappy you were. I've looked it up on the Internet and I think you've got Agoraphobia. It says if it's not cured quickly, it can become a life long problem. Why not ask your GP about it? I'll come with you."

'Oh God! My GP! I'd never gone back to Dr Fox after what happened. I'd always picked up 'the pill' from the local FPA. I was never ill. The Life Insurance Medical had shown both Terry and I had been in perfect health.

"I can't face my GP after all this. I used to work there remember?"

"So what are you going to do Clarice? Do you agree you've got to do something, nip it in the bud. You owe it to Tom."

'I'll have to change my GP,' I thought. But then another idea came to me.

"Your right Jo, I said "I can't go on like this. I know what I'll do. I'll go back to Dr Baverstock. He's the hypnotist who cured me of the fear of flying." Then I thought, 'But I never put flying treatment to the test. Did he really cure me?'

I managed to choke back the tears of what could have been "Would you come with me Jo, for moral support?" I asked.

Dr Baverstock welcomed me again, in the same gentlemanly way as before.

Jo had made the appointment for me, because I couldn't face doing it myself, and had mentioned to Joan, his secretary, that my husband had died.

"My dear," he spoke quietly, "I am so sorry to hear that your husband passed away, recently. Joan told me about your loss. I am so sad for you." He inclined his head and took my arm.

"This way Clarice, come through this way, if you remember?"

He lead me through into the pastel painted, low-lit office.

"Do take a seat, my dear, and make yourself as comfortable as you can," He said gently.

"Thanks so much for seeing me," I began and then I dried up waiting for him to take the initiative.

Seeing I was finding it difficult, he began to speak slowly and quietly, almost as if the hypnosis was already beginning. I could not imagine him ever raising his voice.

"So Clarice, what's brought you here today?" he asked

I looked down at my feet.

"I can't face going out any more!" I blurted out "It was bad enough in the beginning…" He nodded and I continued "I was able to force myself then. I was nervous of going out. But now it's got much worse and can't go out at all. My friend thinks I've got Agoraphobia, she looked it up on the Web."

"Well let's talk about it, shall we?" He continued in his soothing voice "What is it that makes you so afraid? What do you fear will happen to you if you do leave the house?"

"I don't know, that's the trouble! I can't even explain it to myself." I replied

"All right then just tell me what happens to you when you try to go out? What feelings do you start to have while you are preparing to leave?

Do you experience difficulty breathing for instance?"

"Yes, I do and my heart starts to race." I trembled a bit as I explained.

"I feel as if my blood pressures going up and up as if my head's going to burst and my hands go all clammy."

"Good, good." he said "You're explaining yourself really well. Do you get anything like a knot or unpleasant fluttering feelings in your stomach?"

"That's exactly it and I get rushing noises in my head. I can't even hear myself think! I feel as if I'm going to die. The only thing that stops it once it's started is if I change my mind and decide to stay home after all, and then all the feelings start to subside."

"Clarice, you are having panic attacks, my dear, caused by all you have been through recently with the death of your dear husband. Agoraphobia is a condition which builds up slowly over the months and years, and becomes a chronic life time condition It's very hard to treat, but you haven't got it. Your friend was on the right track, the two conditions are linked.

However I'm very glad to tell you that we can completely cure you of your anxiety attacks."

The relief brought a watery smile to my face.

"Today we will start with some breathing techniques, which will help you more and more, as you practise them. Then at our next session, we will do some trance work. Is that alright by you, Clarice?" I nodded

He explained exactly what we were going to do, and by the end of the first set of slow respirations, I started to feel calmer and more relaxed. We continued breathing in unison for a little longer, and I could already feel it was going to help. The doctor himself was sitting with his eyes closed, till we finished. Then as I calmed down, some of my most private feelings about the agonising traumas of my recent past poured out to the good doctor. He sat there quietly, not making any comment, just allowing me to open up to him, till tears trickled down my cheeks. He passed me the tissues and after a little while, said very quietly, that he would see me at the same time the following week. As I left his consulting room I knew that with the help of this gentle, mild mannered man, my panic would evaporate.

Jo conscientiously drove me back and forth for each appointment, and she could see that over the next few weeks the hypnotic sessions were definitely easing my pain, strengthening me and freeing me up to live again.

"Thanks, Jo so much for helping me," I said "I don't know what I would have done without you. I'm beginning to feel like a new woman, thanks to you and Dr B." Jo was thrilled. We started to go shopping together again. The highlight for me was always the coffee shop and the cream buns. I could never resist them!

I started back to the Church again and began to make a few friends among the congregation...acquaintances really, as I never seemed to be able to throw myself properly into the life of the Church. This was the second time Church people had helped me get my life back and I could find no fault with their genuine warmth and friendliness. They all seemed kind and loving, but I always had that sneaking feeling that I was viewed as the stray sheep that needed to be guided back into the fold.

Tom was longing to come home to Debden, though he had loved the break up with his Nan and Trevor, in Chester: a whole new world to him! The two young men, actually uncle and nephew, were great pals, and it was their friendship that had eased Tom's misery after his Dad died. I owed a lot to my brother and, of course, my Mum.

I went up to Mum's to bring Tom back by train, but when I got there he had collected so much extra stuff, with his football kit and new clothes and bags of school books, that Trevor had to drive us back. On the way home, I discovered that Tom had become a football fanatic, playing after school twice a week and watching the local game at weekends. Somehow I had never thought he would be interested in sport. I suppose because Terry hadn't been.

"Mum" he said as soon after we started off "Can you get me a West Ham strip? I'm a West Ham fan now. Their home ground's right near where we live. Well E13. That's near us isn't it? Can you buy me a season ticket for the home games? Pleease."

"Yes, Ok I'm sure we can. How do you know about West Ham anyway? I'd have thought you'd have followed a team nearer your Nan's."

"I've kept in touch with all my mates at school,. Nan thought that would do me good. They all support West Ham. Don't worry she always let me use the phone. It was her idea, And she bought me this." He pulled out a new top of the range mobile, from his pocket.

"Have a look ," he said "It's brilliant. It's got games and a camera. You can even get onto the internet with it."

'Good old Mum,' I thought ' she was better with boys. She knew what made them tick, even now. And she moved with the times. She must have used some of that money I gave her to help with Dad, to buy Tom's mobile. I must remember to transfer some more money into her account, now Dad was in full-time care. He would have the best money could buy, and Mum could have a few treats too, she deserved them!

My Mum!! I felt much better about her now, since she had done so well with Tom, but I still hadn't conquered how I felt about her. Deep down there was something I couldn't get over. I couldn't just love her unconditionally. Ah well! Till I knew what it was, I would make sure she had everything money could buy.

Chapter 11

Tom had really come out of himself, since he had been trailing round with the Trevor. I was very glad to have him back home. Life now seemed as complete as it could ever be, since losing Terry.

But Tom wasn't satisfied with his friends, football and being at home with me. He wanted a dog. I think he missed a male influence in the house, and perhaps a hound would go some way to filling the bill.

Snuffles became his constant companion. We rescued him from Battersy dogs home. It was such a difficult decision. As we passed down the corridors that housed the dogs' cages, each dog eyed us soulfully, hoping it would be chosen, then as we walked on past, it turned away, resigned. That is until Tom saw Snuffles. He was halfway in size between a Jack Russell and a Retriever, a mixture of orangey brown hair with black spodges. But he had a tufty fringe of hair round his mouth and eye brows reminiscent of a Shih Tzu. I would have loved to have met his parents! Tom had all sorts of more complimentary dog names up his sleeve, but the new addition did snuffle, especially when he tucked in to his dinner, so 'Snuffles' stuck.

We had prepared a wicker basket for him, lined with a soft material and a special doggie cushion, but after that first night he always slept in or on Tom's bed.

Tom started to take an interest in school work for the first time and did well in the GCSE mocks, and much to my amazement got a number of A*s for the real thing. He chose Science to study for A level, Physics and Chemistry plus Computer Technology. The teachers were thrilled with his work and told me so at open night.

I bought him a new laptop for his studies and the old tower, sit-up-and-beg computer was relegated to me, Tom set up an email account for me and showed me how to surf the web for information. Previously, at Willow Green, I had only been able to input patients' details and use the word processor for typing, so this opened up a whole new world for me.

With Tom engaged in football, dog walking and swatting, I found a friend in the computer, preferring to play games on it in the evenings to watching endless 'Soaps' and depressing News rounds and political debates on the Tele.

At last, I classed myself as sane.

I was able to go out and about on my own.

I got much more involved with the church, making cakes to be sold at bazaars and fetes, Gathering jumble for sales to make money for the cubs and scouts.

I even helped at the weekly welfare club for the elderly.

Despite all my involvement, nothing changed my mind about the church.

I liked the friendship and the love and kindness that emanated from most of its members; yet I knew that I could never really be one of them. I think Jo and Rod knew how I felt, but as they believed their Lord could work wonders in the heart of even the toughest unbeliever, so they continued to try hard with me.

At last, I made myself go up, with Tom, to visit Mum, but it wasn't until Dad died. Everyone was rather relieved that he had slipped away in his sleep.

Soon after that, Prue got married. I went up for this occasion too. She got married as everyone had long expected, but not to the rather greasy Phil. Callam was the lucky bridegroom. He certainly had more to say for himself than Phil and, as mum said, had 'better prospects'!

My heart was always heavy without Terry, but otherwise life was as good as it could be. Tom was doing brilliantly all round, with his football, his school work and his mates and last but not least, Snuffles, who had become as dear to me, as he was to Tom.

Then, two things happened to rock my boat. The first was the arrival, at last, of Terry's Life insurance money. The company had delayed paying out and argued about it for a very long time, because they thought it odd that there had been such a short interval between Terry taking out the insurance, and his death. I suppose they were trying to work out if Terry had purposely put himself in the path of the killer-crane. Hardly likely, when he was weeks away from the longed for trip to Barbados, but to be fair, stranger things happen. To them 'Terry Smith' was only a name on a form. They didn't know how much he loved me and Tom, and how much he wanted to stay alive. Because of the delay in settlement, I had put the matter completely out of my mind, totally forgotten about it, so when the money came through, Terry's death hit me afresh, just as if it had been yesterday. It was huge amount of money. Blood money! My Terry, in exchange for hundreds of thousands of pounds.

It sickened me.

The second occurrence was worse. It shocked me and turned my bones to jelly.

It was only a text, just a few abbreviated, misspelled words on my mobile phone. Nevertheless it made me shudder!

'So sad re ur loss. U no im here 4 u & we cn go on as b4 xxx J'

The first thing I did was ring up a local husband and wife medical partnership and register as a patient of Dr Sarah Evans. It was only a gesture of defiance. I didn't need a doctor at that moment, but I wanted to cut off completely from the Health Centre and never risk setting eyes on that awful man again

The second thing I did was vomit.

That night, my bingeing re-started with a vengeance.

It was the one thing I had never mentioned to Dr Baverstock, or indeed to anyone. It was my secret. It was such a part of me and it always helped me out when things went wrong. I'd be lost without it, I didn't want to be cured, at least not while I could control my weight in my time-honoured way.

The late night feasting restarted and became a regular event. I hadn't done it properly since I'd worked as nanny with Kathy's family. Oh well, old habits die hard!

I ordered more and more rich food from Tesco... Cakes and pastries full-cream yoghurts, dairy ice cream by the bucketful. Sausage rolls and multipacks of crisps. Now, I didn't have to traipse round the shops anymore or struggle to carry it all home. Tesco's van didn't mind how many times a week it delivered to our house. Best of all I didn't need to count the pennies, I was rolling in money.

The orders were much bigger than a single adult and her nearly grown teenage son could possibly put away, but Tesco didn't query it!

I gorged the sweetest, creamiest foods I could lay my hands on, every night, till I was fit to burst and then vomited it all up and went to sleep. It became a deeply ingrained pattern, which repeated itself night after night for months. I was addicted to the drug 'food'. I was as addicted to food as my father had been to alcohol: Though he only vomited by default.

Somehow, instead of it making me feel guilty and upset, as it had before, all it did now was ease the pain of my loss. I felt cleansed and invigorated, Terry would be pleased that I could keep my trim figure. Following the dreadful upset of his death, I had been too consumed with grief to eat properly and my weight had slipped away to 8 ½ stone and I'd looked a bit gaunt, or so people said. Now, I aimed to keep it that way. But I could still eat to my heart's content. I patted myself on the back! I really did have the secret to keeping slim!

Jo seemed to sense there was something seriously wrong with me.

She came round one day, leaving Meg with a friend.

"Look Clarice" she said, "I don't think you're very well. Why not forget about hypnosis and go and see a counsellor, or a therapist?"

I knew more than she could ever know that she was right. I was forced to admit to myself, that things were getting out of hand, this time. My secret was out of my control!

That's when I found Grace's number in 'Yellow pages' listed under Psychologists. I couldn't help noticing that the heading above was 'Psychics and Clairvoyants'! After Odessa, I wouldn't be consulting one of those again in a hurry...I wondered if she had ever joined her operatic lover, or whether she was she still reading hands in her silky boudoir?

My hunt for peace began again.

Grace was a tall, thin, rather plain woman, with a face that didn't give a thing away. She had a calm but neutral air about her. I didn't take to her the minute I set eyes on her, but I wasn't sure why. There was nothing not to like.

At the first session, Grace told me that all my present problems dated back to my 'wounded inner child'

That was her speciality. She believed that everything that bugs us during every part of our adult life,is due to how we were treated as kids. 'Well fine, that sounds a reasonable assumption.' I thought, 'I'll give it a go.'

I tried to tell her about Terry's death. How the anguish of it kept coming back to me. That just when I thought things were getting better, something would come 'out of the blue' to flummox me again.

"Life's just gone down hill and become unbearable since Terry went." I began, my eyes prickling with tears.

She let me go all through my story again, and then she said "Clarice, I can see how upset you are over your loss,

I'm not belittling it, but I think the fact that you've taken so long to recover from Terry's death has a much deeper cause. This ongoing grief has to do with your childhood." I began to realise why I hadn't engaged with her in the beginning. She was ice-cold.

"Tell me about your early life."

Now through gushing tears, which no amount of tissue could soak up, I told her, about Dad's drinking, with Mum trying to keep up appearances and give Trevor the special care he needed. I told her that Dad had wanted me to be a boy, he had told me that repeatedly during my early life.

"If you'd been a boy Clarice everything would have been different. A boy first to start the family off, that's what we should have had. Then everything would have been different.

He'd repeat it over and over, especially when he'd been drinking. But that was common wasn't it?" I looked at Grace for her agreement on that point. Her face was expressionless. "I'd heard it from other girls at school anyway." I continued "Then, after me came another girl, but Prue still became his favourite, even though she was a girl too, because Trevor was damaged. I was just the fat, ugly work-horse with buck teeth. More my Mum's assistant than her cherished little girl." I looked up and realised I'd come out with more than I'd intended. Actually I'd never really put all this into words before, even in my mind.

Suddenly I saw it all, but I didn't need **her** to explain it to me. I had always known, deep down, as most people from dysfunctional families know, that my childhood had been, indirectly at least, the cause of all my problems. I didn't need **her** to tell me! Everything would have been alright if Terry had lived and we had gone on together, into old age. I wasn't dumb. I knew 'all God's children got problems'. I had read somewhere that ninety something percent of people come from 'dysfunctional' families, anyway. But that wasn't as bad as some poor kids had it, struggling for survival, in some god-forsaken parts of the world, where there's no running water, no crops growing to be harvested. What I'd suffered was nothing like as bad as being brought up in an HIV-endemic zone, where errant soldiers might cut off your arms and legs or rape you, soon as look at you! Where had this woman been all her life? She was…prissy, that was the word. Now I knew why I didn't like her.

"You see," said Grace "you missed out on the unconditional love every child should have. You have a void that needs to be filled. This is the hunger of the wounded inner child. You **are** your own darling little inner child, Clarice. You suffered such extreme emptiness which you could have filled with drugs or alcohol, but you chose to fill it with food."

"Yes," I agreed.

Food was my drug and my escape. I'd known that all along. My escape from an upbringing where tears had not been allowed and hugs were absent.

"No, no I was never abused?" I said in answer to her next question.

"Yes, Clarice you were abused. Your mother expected you to be her little helper and her moral support. She used **you** to comfort **her**, when it should have been the other way round."

"Oh, I see what you mean," I said.

"Clarice ,how did your father react to you?"

"What do you mean, react?"

"Well, as you said you were the first girl and then Prudence. He'd had to wait till the third child to get a boy."

"Her name's Prue," I corrected, but I still didn't answer the question; partly because I didn't know how to answer it, and partly because she was starting to get my goat.

"What happened at school Clarice? You mentioned on the phone that you'd been bullied?"

"Yes, that's what the headmistress called it.

"Tell me what happened?"

"Well the other kids called me names, the girls mostly. Said I was fat and ugly. Said I had big teeth. But I never cried about it. I never let it get to me."

"Was that because your dad had stopped you crying at home?"

"No. It was my mum. She caught me looking in the mirror once, when I was howling, tears pouring down my face and she said "Go on Clarice, go on cry! that's right **cry**! Look at yourself. What a sight!" So, after that, I didn't cry any more. Not often anyway."

She looked at me, waiting "Oh yes" I continued and if I ever did cry, which was hardly ever, she'd say "Shut up crying Clarice, or I'll give you something to cry about!" I looked up at Grace.

"So it wasn't your Dad who was so unkind to you?"

"No, because he was usually out of it with drink." I said "but I really loved my Mum." I added.

"Yes I know you did, Clarice," She answered.

"The point is Clarice you loved your Mum despite how much she upset and used you." I nodded "and you loved your Dad even though he was too drunk to care for you properly. That is, care like a Dad should. He wasn't 'there' for you. Am I right, Clarice?" I nodded again

"Parents need to be able to listen quietly to what their children say, and not shut them up. They should let their children play and have fun, not put them to work as house-maids. Parents who don't fulfil their proper role, end up with children who become addicts."

Grace said I had a 'spiritual wound' which I was filling with food. So whenever I was very sad, for whatever reason and needed healing, I ate.

"When you feel really bad what do you always do, Clarice."

"I eat "I replied "I eat till I'm numb."

"And then ?" she asked

"I eat till I'm full, and then I, I...I vomit." I stammered. This was the first time I had ever told anyone my secret." I felt the blood leave my face. My head began to swim. Why **do** you vomit, Clarice? She asked . I put my hand up in a vain attempt to shield my face. "To stay thin." I answered

"Is that the only reason?"

"No, I have to cleanse myself."

What from?"

"From guilt."

"It's not your guilt, Clarice. That guilt belongs to your family. Your mum and dad. Eventually you will be able to forgive them, But first you need to heal yourself.

You have to allow your feelings to come through. All these years you've had to swallow your feelings, so in adult life, you've swallowed food instead, to stop those painful feelings in their tracks. You didn't have a healthy role model as a child. Nobody ever listened to 'little Clarice', so the stress grew and grew till it became unbearable. Chronic stress leads to depression. In the end, all that's left is a big hole that constantly needs filling."

I nodded again.

"When you were a child you had no one to listen to you; No one to ease your emotional pain. Now you don't need to look for another person, to heal that life-long pain, the healing has to come from within yourself. You have to go back as 'Clarice, the adult' and hug 'Clarice, the little girl', the damaged child. You need to tell her that you'll always be there for her. So when Little Clarice's memories of hurt come through to you, take yourself back in time, in your mind, and hug her. Love her as she was never loved in the past. Do you understand what I am saying?" I must have looked a bit blank, but nodded and managed to produce a glimmer of a polite smile.

"Well that's all we have time for today, Clarice. I'll see you in two weeks."

She held out her hand which I shook.

"Goodbye. Clarice." she said "Think through all we've talked about, before we meet again. Next time, we'll discuss how you can learn to comfort that inner child, properly." She smiled. "Could you phone up for your next appointment? I haven't got my diary here, and my secretary's off this afternoon." I nodded and smiled again.

After leaving Grace's consulting room, I hopped into Jo's car beaming.

"Well how did you get on?" she asked. "you look as though you've won the lottery! Oh sorry I forgot, just a turn of phrase." She laughed apologetically."

"Well how was it, anyway?"

"Great!" I said, "I've come to my senses. I realise what a self indulgent fool I've been!"

What ever do you mean, Clarice, you were ill?" She said "Wrong Jo, I was being totally selfish and self absorbed!" She raised her eye brows. "The idea of me, a bright young widow, with a healthy, sporty teenage son and pots of money, should start moaning to some professional shrink about a few small incidents in my childhood. It's ridiculous. I felt like a right sick cow in there!"

"Why what happened? What did she say? What was it like?" Asked Jo

"Look Jo, I can't go over it all now. It's a lot of complicated rubbish! But thanks so much for driving me. Let's go and have a cup of tea, if you've got time before picking Meg up?"

"Nothing but the best, darling!" I giggled, as she tried to pull up outside a MacDonald's, and then added, "We need a proper tea shop with pretty table cloths and bone china." Jo knew just where to take us. I wished I had learned to drive, it obviously helps so much to get to know a town. I only got to know the shops between bus stops!

Over tea, I steered the conversation away from everything to do with therapy, especially the events of the afternoon. I wanted to sift through my outpourings with Grace later on, when I was quite alone. Luckily for me, Jo was dying to tell me that she was pregnant again, and that she and Rod were both very excited about the forth coming birth. Perhaps Tom would like to be one of the baby's prayer partners? I managed not to blush as I remembered that I hadn't taken up that role for dear little Meg.

"You'd better ask Tom nearer the time." I said. (I would warn him in advance so that he would know what to say when she did ask.) They had decided to have another baby quickly as Meg was toddling and they thought that she would love a sibling to play with!...I wasn't sure of this, but said nothing.

I wanted to repay Jo for some of her kindness to me, and she always looked drained, so I promised her that we would go for a day at the Spa (if she knew where that was?) and she could have massages and any treatment applicable for a pregnant woman. She was absolutely thrilled. I'd never done much to help her, I'd not even baby-sat for her. This was a little gift in return.

I suddenly felt I wanted to give her some special treats, to make up for the past. After we had talked baby talk in all it's aspects for a while, the conversation inevitably turned to the church, the crèche, the Sunday school, and the Bible study group she and Rod had started to hold in their home once a week. This was the church's latest attempts at outreach. For Jo, it was a treat in itself for me to let her ramble on about the church, as after Meg and Rod, it was the subject nearest to her heart. In the past, I had usually tried to steer her conversation away from the goings on at St Winnifred's, but today it suited me to let her chatter on about her favourite subject, and it certainly pleased her.

After tea she dropped me home and I started to think.

Actually, I did a hundred and one other things, some unnecessary, before I made myself sit down to think, it was all so painful.

My first decision was not to phone for a further appointment to see Grace.

I could understand and accept a lot of what she had said as true. But it was none of her business. She seemed like a like a surgeon who would gradually dissect my life and examine all my diseased parts, and tell me which bits were good enough to keep. Actually no! She was more like a morbid anatomist who would stuff all my organs back in, diseased or otherwise, and then write me a report on her findings. I didn't like her one little bit. She gave me the creeps, nothing like dear old Dr

Baverstock. I'd stick to him if I needed help in the future. He was such a dear old soul, so soothing, you could say anything to him and not feel embarrassed.

Grace, the psychotherapist, talked of my past abuse, but that's almost how she made me feel in her presence, my mind peeled raw. I felt naked and abused all over again. What had Richard Bandler called her sort? Pscho-the-rapist!

That was it. She'd raped my mind!

My second decision was to grow up and use my own determination. I acted like a kid compared to the sensible Jo.

I thought again, as I told Jo, in the tea shop. Life wasn't all that bad. I would start to count my blessings. I had my lovely Tom. Jo and Rod were my best friends and I knew lots of other people in the Church. I had plenty of money to play with and start to help others with, and lastly, I shared our highly desirable dog, Snuffles.

I **would** restrict my eating. Write out a sensible weekly menu and factor in a certain number of treats. Knock vomiting on the head, that whole binge/vomit cycle was finished. My teeth would soon rot away with the gastric acid if I continued. Go back to the Gym and do some working out. Increase my muscle to fat ratio. Get a tan, maybe spray-on. Have a good hair cut, get some high lights. May be someone would take a fancy to me, but he would have to be single, honest, good-hearted and open. No complications! Someone who could befriend a fatherless teenager and his dog! It was now over two years since Terry's accident. He would be pleased I was moving on.

After a Pilates session at the gym, while I was having a cup of tea with some of the girls, one of them said that she had joined an online dating site. She sounded really excited, and said she'd been shown a lot of interest.

I was fascinated. It was something I had never thought of for myself, though I'd often heard it advertised on local radio.

After most of the others had dispersed, I introduced myself to the girl who had mentioned online dating

"Hi," I said "I'm Clarice,I couldn't help hearing what you were saying about dating sites, earlier on."

"It's Lynne" she said by way of introduction, "What do you want to know?"

Lynne seemed thrilled to pour out all the information and then went on to tell me about her successes on 'There's someone for everyone.com'.

"Thanks a million" I said "I'll give it a go!"

"You won't be sorry" said Lynne as she turned to go, "See you next week."

On the bus going home, I thought 'I **will** give it a go! Why not? What have I got to lose?'

It was time to move on. Tom already had. For the first few weeks at Mum's, after Terry's death, he wept into his pillow every night over the terrible blow of losing his Dad. Terry had been a top father. The two, father and son, were buddies. At weekends, they had always done things together. Tom mourned that closeness. He also mourned what might have been. The promise of our first foreign holiday all together, as a family, and of travelling to all the other places we'd talked of visiting. Tom had been looking forward so much to Egypt, in the Autumn. But Mum had done the job of comforting him. It should have been my job, but I was incapable. She had helped him through the bereavement period then, gradually, Trevor had taken over.

Trevor was the one who had got him interested in football, been to matches with him, and took over the role of buddie from Terry. My brother and mother had both done a fantastic job, and with the resilience of youth Tom, had moved on from the terrible sadness, while never forgetting his Dad.

Now it was my turn to move on. I went upstairs and logged into the computer. Without Terry, it was mine exclusively.

First, I searched for dating sites and then I remembered the name of Lynne's one. ' There's someone for everyone.com', so I joined that one. She seemed delighted with the results and said she had been on a few dates already!

The home page was cluttered with hearts and pictures of cupids, and offered 'One month's free membership'. I'd already decided to join, if only for a laugh, but I still liked a bargain. There was a list of pretty intrusive questions. I hadn't thought of this. I had always hated giving anyone my personal details, but in for a penny... I could always lie,and I supposed some people did? But what was the point. Date of birth? That was the worst one. I was nearly 36. Where had all those years gone? They also wanted to me to write a short paragraph about myself ,

So I wrote ' I am a slim and fair haired. Recently widowed with a teenage son. We also have a friendly dog. I go to the gym to keep fit, and sometimes go to the Anglican church . My hobby is cooking. I'm looking for fun and friendship, perhaps leading to something more.'

Reading it though, I could see that I was short on hobbies, but maybe Mr Right would hope that he could become my main hobby? I deleted 'recent', from 'recent widow', in case they thought I wasn't over it. (Well, in a sense I never would be.) I had put Anglican in to show I wasn't a 'holy Roman' or a 'Bible basher' but I substituted the word 'spiritual'. So now my self portrait read:- 'I am a slim fair widow with a teenage son and his dog. I try to keep fit at the Gym and am interested in spiritual things. Cooking is one of my hobbies. I am looking for friendship and fun with the right person.'

I sent in the best photo I could find by post, as I didn't know how to 'upload' a photo, and I didn't want to ask Tom!

I was given a password, which I obviously can't divulge and a code name to silly for me to repeat!

After all that, which was quite draining, I flicked through some of the pictures of eligible males, and seeing nothing that appealed to me, I logged off, grabbed a sandwich and went to bed.

I was so tired I thought that I would fall asleep immediately. But images of Grace began to float through my mind, as soon as my eyes closed.

'Grace', I had never known the exact definition of that word. Grace was one of the Christian virtues. To me it meant dignity, charm and kindness all rolled into one. What a poor choice of name for her. Her parents had probably thought that their sweet, chubby, little girl would grow up into a charming, kindly woman! Well how wrong they had been. I found Grace austere to the point of arrogance: Intrusive into me. She went where I hadn't invited her. She didn't ask my opinion, but told me what we were going to do. She was so unbendingly sure of herself.

Well, I wouldn't be going back for a second appointment. She got that wrong!

I didn't like people who made me cry.

Chapter 12

After dismissing Grace, the luckless inner child therapist, finally from my mind, I sunk into a deeply refreshing, dreamless sleep.

The next morning, after I had packed Tom off to school with his football kit slung over one arm and his laptop gripped under the other, I raced up stairs, two at a time, and logged in to see if I had collected any admirers.

No, how disappointing! I guessed that was because my photo hadn't yet been posted on the site. I scanned the list of available men. They had to be within striking distance as I couldn't drive, free from baggage and taller than me, or at least the same height; and of course, extremely attractive! I didn't want much! After looking through rows and rows of photos of men looking for 'lurve', I lost concentration and decided to go down and take Snuffles out for his morning constitutional, to clear my head.

It wouldn't be a long walk today, just round the block and back, as I wanted to get back and study the 'wannabees'. But when I got out into the fresh morning, with the sun just beginning to take the chill off the air, I decided to follow Snuffles' lead. He was so excited jumping up and down, and as soon as I unclipped his leash he raced on down to the field, where Tom always took him. I followed him over the style and he bounded away into the distance to hunt for rabbit holes. He did stop once to turn and make sure I was following, and then continued on his own private adventure. Tom had trained him to come when he was called, so I was free to amble at my own pace and take in the scenery. I couldn't remember the last time I had felt so free and relaxed. There was so much to see that I hadn't noticed before. My old angst-ridden self, must have previously deleted the beautiful green, scrubby hedges, the trees, breaking into bud already. An early Spring this year? The sun was shining in the palest blue sky. A great happiness swept over me. Tom and Snuffles were my two darlings, now. Did I really want a third person coming into my life at this time? Someone who would, at the very least, interfere with my newly found peace, and might, in the worst case scenario, cause utter chaos.

Home at last, a temporarily worn-out Snuffles, made straight for his basket to gnaw his old bone before his mid-morning nap. With nothing better to do, I took a big cup of coffee upstairs to the computer. I felt very diffident now about the whole dateline thing, but curiosity got the better of me and I thought I might scan the faces again, in case I'd missed anything! No need! There, in the middle of the screen was a flashing message. It read 'You have mail!'

Barclay appeared to be a true gentleman. He took me out to an expensive restaurant attached to a Wine Merchants, in Epping.

White starched tablecloths and serviettes in fluted glasses. Waitresses in black dresses and starched white aprons, looking like old fashioned maids.

Quite impressive!

He tasted the wine as requested by the wine waiter, which annoyed me. I was a new woman and this was a hangover from the past.

Barclay told me his life story. I listened. My session with Grace had taught me the truth of the old Bible saying, 'Not to cast my pearls before swine.' I wasn't sure yet what category Barclay fell into. Was he just 'posh' or would he turn out to be a cad?

Barclay's first wife, who had raised their children and run the house, while he worked as an executive, sadly died of a devastating cancer, while still young.

So, he told me, he obtained, (by fair means or foul) a wife from the Orient, who had, according to his description, doubled as a housekeeper and general dog's body.

It emerged that they had fallen out over their respective children. His were, by all accounts, bright and rich. Hers, apparently much less so. Gradually he began to feel that her family were becoming a needy embarrassment. As she missed her kids so much, he enabled her emigrate to Australia. Where her son lived. He obtained an iffy visa by 'speaking to some one in high places. Basically, he'd paid her off.

"Unfortunately ," he said, looking at me with a shy smile "We aren't yet divorced. But that can be arranged quite quickly. It shouldn't hold things up."

He told me that he had been head of the Rotary club and it transpired that his politics were right of right. He owned a luxury yacht anchored in Marbella. He said that he could take me over there, in a few weeks time, for a fortnight's holiday, if I liked.

"What do you do all day, over there?" I asked"

"I just potter around, chatting to all the locals. But you could lie on the deck, in your bikini," he smirked "getting a lovely tan"

"But, what would I **do** all day?" I asked

"Well, my dear," he repilied "you could read all the paperbacks you liked, and in between you could go for a swim to cool off."

"And in the evening?" I asked

"We'll go round to all the little wine bars and fish restaurants, together, and eat at a different one each evening."

"How nice!" I said

"Of course, he added, "some off the time, my son and his wife will be out there with us. We bought the yacht together, as an investment, and now we think of it as our bolthole."

In the candle light, after several glasses of wine, I could see the allure.

When we met again, later in the week for lunch, he looked a lot older and I knew he had lied about his age. As we walked to Café Uno, he leaned heavily on his furled golf umbrella, which he said he had brought along, "as it looked like rain".

During lunch, Barclay asked me if I would accompany him to see an amateur stage show. His grandchildren had leading parts. If I agreed, he would buy the tickets. I thanked him, and as we parted, and promised I would check my diary and let him know about the show.

Once home, I thought about the yacht parked up in Marbella, where I would be bored out of my skull, reading novels all day. I'd never been a great reader anyway! And where was Tom in all this. He hadn't been mentioned, though Barclay must have read my resume and known I had a son. I didn't need to check my diary, I knew it was empty.

I logged on and wrote him a carefully worded email.

It read :- 'Dear Barclay, thank you so much for taking me out to dinner and then to lunch. It was very nice to meet you and hear your story. I have thought about things carefully and don't think we are entirely compatible, so I won't be able to come and watch your grandchildren perform. Thank you for asking, All the best in your continued search for happiness, I wish you well, Clarice'

An email came back at once - 'Clarice, I'm devastated! I thought it was all settled between us. I have told my children all about you and they were thrilled and looking forward to meeting you at the show. Please say you will reconsider. I think we are perfectly suited, Barclay.'

What was he on?! Was he so used to getting his own way, that I was just a fait accompli? Thank God I hadn't given him my phone number!

The next email was from Carl. He started work in the Merchant Navy, and later he took a job helping to raise the Marie Celeste. At present he was a dog walker in the USA. He admitted to being penniless, but said loved the carefree life and eked out a living from walking celebrities' pet pooches and doing some semi-professional photography. He sent me some beautiful photos of the Grand Canyon and one of him. He did look tall and handsome in the photo, but when he uncoiled himself from his hired Smart car on his visit to me, he appeared very different. Firstly, he was puffing and blowing from his bad chest, a legacy from working in the boiler rooms on the Merchant ships, and secondly he was nothing like his photo, which he later admitted he'd 'touched up'. He didn't appeal at all, but unfortunately he had driven down from the North, and it was too far for him to return that night! After supper, he tried to tempt me with his pencil-thin winkle, not even thick enough to be described as a dick, but I declined, and sent him scurrying to the spare room.

Lucky I did, because a week later he emailed me to, say he'd come out in Herpes. Another lucky escape!

However despite realising quite quickly that I wasn't going to let another man into our household, which, after all was Tom's domain as much as mine, I thought it would be fun to go on a few dates, as long as I obeyed the rules suggested by the dating site. We were told to meet up the first time in a public place, have our mobiles to hand, and tell a friend where we are going. Jo was the only person I could think of to trust, but I knew that if I did tell her where I was going, she would disapprove. So I would keep my mobile at hand anyway, to use if there was any trouble. I just wanted to see how the dating scene had changed over the years, since I'd met Terry.

The next email was from Jeff in Jersey. He said he was an accountant who lived with his aged mother, and found it difficult to get away. Would I like to fly over and he would pick me up from Jersey airport. He sounded cultured, but it meant staying at least one night to make the distance and expense worthwhile. He assured me that he would book me in at the local B&B, and I was nearly convinced, till he started to discuss my black lacy underwear! Could I bring mine with me? As his chat became more salacious, I rumbled him, and suggested he got onto a specialised phone line where someone would be happy to discuss his pervy preferences, at a price.

I began to wonder if the wording of my profile was enticing weirdos. I made a memo to myself to ask Lynne how she was getting on with her dates, next time I saw her at the gym.

Ben was nice. He had a lovely smile, but told me he was very quiet, and had a problem making conversation. On the grounds that he had been too recently widowed and owned a long haired German Shepherd, which might have eaten Snuffles alive, I crossed him off my list of possibles.

Fergus described himself as an 'HR Manager' I was too ignorant to know what HR stood for, and kept thinking 'Her Royal what? Majesty?'

We met in a Loughton wine bar. I looked for the rugged, hairy, outward bound young man of his photo, but it wasn't till everyone else had settled at a table, that I noticed the oldish, bald man in a Fair Isle jumper, holding up the bar. He was the only single man left. I went over to enquire.

"Hi, I'm Clarice. Are you Fergus?" he kissed me as he said "Yes" and I had to dodge the wet lips, by deftly turning my cheek.

His aim was to fuck me, come what may.

As I hadn't been very forthcoming, at the first couple of meetings; though he did manage to force his tongue briefly into my mouth each time we parted, he tried another tactic. On the third date, at a pub near where I lived, he spiked my drink. I arrived by bus and he was already sitting at one of the bar tables with a glass of red wine in front of him. We exchanged 'hellos' and I asked him if he could get me a drink.

"Sure, what do you want, Clarice?"

"Dry, white wine, please." I replied

When he got to the bar he ordered the drink, with his back turned towards me, so that I couldn't see exactly what he was doing. He was taking ages. When he returned to his seat, he didn't bring my glass of wine with him. After a moment, I said "I thought you were getting me a drink? Where is it?" He looked vague and said, "Oh yes, I'll go and get it"

I watched as he took his time, his back still turned against me. Later, I realised he must have been waiting for whatever it was to dissolve.

As soon as I started to drink the wine I began to feel weird. Wine never affected me like this. I was quite used to it. I drank it down, not realising what was happening. Maybe it was just its affect on an empty stomach.

"Clarice, he said "Shall we go and sit down the other end of the pub where it's quieter, this music is getting on my nerves." 'Shame,' I thought I loved the music and gaiety of everyone laughing and chatting, it reminded me of those nights out with Nic and Lara. We moved down to the other end of the pub and he brought me a second glass of wine. This time it tasted quite different and had little further effect on me, though I still felt odd from the first glass.

He **had** to drive me home. I was too 'out of it' to catch a bus. I hadn't wanted him to find out where I lived. Unfortunately it was Friday night and Tom was at a friend's sleep-over.

I offered him coffee when we got in, but he said he wasn't thirsty. He sat down and pulled me down beside him on the sofa, and in my dazed mood he managed to push his fat, meaty his tongue, as far down my throat as he could, repeatedly. It was horrible. I couldn't speak. He started to feel me all over, putting his hand up my skirt. He stopped 'kissing' to take my hand, and he forced it down his trousers, telling me to stroke his turgid penis. It was disgusting. As he unzipped, I managed to stand up and shout at him to get out. "No" he said "you can't do that. You've egged me on. You can't prick tease me like that."

With my fight and flight response giving me a surge of adrenaline, I ran to the front door and literally booted him out. If he had turned round, I would have kneed him in the crutch. I don't know where I got the strength from. As he revved up the car, he shouted out of the window "I'm going to make you regret this Clarice."

I was shaking when he left. What I couldn't understand though was, why hadn't he spiked my second drink. Did he take fright. Or was he worried that with too much of the drug inside me, he'd never have been able to get me into his car to bring me home?

I bolted the door that night. It did worry me somewhat, that he knew where I lived, but I'd typed a lot of insurance reports and business letters, during my past life as a medical secretary, and decided an attempted Rape charge would not look good on the CV of 'Human Resources Manager' (I'd looked up the meaning of 'HR' on Google) Next day I emailed him :-"Fergus, did you spike my drink last night?" I never got a reply. I wasn't expecting one, but I just wanted him to know he'd been rumbled.

It was depressing. Either there were no half-decent fun men out there or I had been very unlucky. I was on the point of giving up when another message came through. It looked more interesting as the man lived near, and owned a business. Someone of some standing in society, I thought. I'll just give this dating thing one more go. Colin swept up to the front gate in a flash sports car. Tom, who was watching from the dining room window, raised his eyebrows with a 'Wow' escaping from his lips. It was unusual to see my son impressed. He was staying in that night so, for the first time, some one knew where I was going and who I was going with.

Colin was dressed in cord trousers and an open-necked shirt. He was tall and pleasant looking, but I noticed he had a bit of a beer gut.

"Hello Clarice" he leered, or was it my imagination. My index of suspicion had risen over the last few weeks. Tom waved from the front door, "Bye Mum. Have a good evening."

As soon as we sat down in the Curry house and started on our Poppadoms, Colin started to unburden himself about his past life. He was well-spoken, a man of the world, but as soon as he told me he had three ex-wives, I wrote him off, He wove an almost believable hard luck tale as we washed our curries down with Cobra. I was slightly intrigued, despite myself.

The next date was to be at his house not too far down the road from mine. He was going to cook supper. Well that was great, because although my bulimia was gone, courtesy of Grace, I still loved home cooked food. The pork cutlets, were grilled to a crisp, because his dog had done a whoopsy under the table while he was at the stove, and he had to abandon the cooking to clear it up.

"Well don't look at me I said. I can't bear the smell!"

He was annoyed. Partly with himself for not letting the dog out in time, partly with me for not helping. The evening was going downhill fast.

He put on the TV and together we watched a slightly titillating serial, while he sat at my feet stroking my leg and trying to go up further. The minute the program ended, I stood up to leave, but he grabbed me and kissed me ferociously.

I tried to pull away. "What are you doing," he said "You know you want to."

I didn't stay to find out what he presumed he knew I wanted to do, but tore out of the house and ran most of the way home. It wasn't far, but quite far enough. I was winded when I got home.

I had learnt my lesson properly this time. I decided to give up internet dating, altogether, but out of sheer curiosity, I couldn't resist logging on to the site from time to time, just to see what was on offer.

I felt I needed to warn other women about the dangers of internet dating. It appeared that at their best these men were often incapable of charming women in real life, and so had to resort to hiding behind a screen. These two-dimensional internet Romeos were, at best, quite devoid of insight and at worst, very dangerous.

Chapter 13

My biggest commitment for now was going to be Tom. He had done so well at school in Essex since coming back to me from Chester. In year 12 he had started his A level course in earnest, Biology, Chemistry and IT. I secretly wondered whether he would apply for a medical or veterinary course at university. With the help of his teachers at school, he had gone through all the possibilities. I didn't mind what course he decided on, but hoped against hope that he would choose a local college. Selfishly, I wanted him to stay near to me, but deep inside I knew he wanted to move back up North near to Trevor. We didn't discuss it because we were so close, and each of us secretly knew that whatever was said might upset the other.

Trevor had been his rock, like an older brother to him after Terry died, while I had gone to pieces and not been there for him. Tom was eighteen now and, I realised that in some ways he needed to cut loose from my apron strings.

No pressure was put on him. At open evening, his teachers said he was very bright and could take his pick of courses. They predicted straight 'A's.

Eventually, he did tell me that he had applied to three university colleges, Brighton, Kent, down in Canterbury, and Chester, but he still wanted to ask my advice on what course he could do.

I just listened and thought I would know from his expression which appealed to him most.

"I'm torn between Biology and Biomedical Sciences," he said "Which do you think?" "I've decided to give up IT, after this year," he added. "Too many nerds doing it, I wouldn't stand a chance of getting a job after College."

"What sort of job would Biology set you up for than?" I asked

"Well I could be a lab. assistant or a medical technician. If I did biomedical studies I could end up as a doctor! How would you like that, Mum? You could be end up being my medical secretary!" he laughed.

"I'd probably be retired before you got your private practice!" I smiled at the idea.

"There is just one other possibility." He said tentatively.

"What's that?" I asked

"Well, I've looked it up, and there is a course at Chester on 'Animal management', you only need, 260 UCAS points including a C in Biology! It's only a foundation course, but it lasts two years. You know how I love animals, Mum. I could apply for the Biology degree after that," he was in the zone now and was talking faster and faster, his face alive with excitement, "or, "he paused, looking at me to watch my reaction, "Or, after the foundation course, I could apply to Veterinary College and be a Vet instead? What d'ya think?" he ended triumphantly. He was grinning from ear to ear. I threw my arms round him to give him the biggest cuddle and we jigged round the living room I like a couple of dements. Snuffles took one look at us and so as not to be left out, leapt from his basket right up between the two of us, into Tom's arms and then we all had a group love-in.

Tom's relief was palpable. He had obviously been sitting on these ideas, wondering whether or not to tell me, trying to pre-guess my response. The air had been cleared and I was truly delighted for him. How proud Terry would have been!

Over the summer, Tom went out a lot with his mates, but we still shared some good times together. Rambles in the woods with Snuffles, and BBQs in the garden, my friends mixing with his, over burnt sausages and 'fruit cup' usually strongly laced with vodka, which one of Tom's many girl friends always seemed to carry in her backpack! The best time of the summer, was when we went with Jo, Rod and Meg, on a day trip to St Leonards-on-sea. It touched me to see Tom play in the sand with Meg, building her little castles which she took great pleasure in knocking down. Sitting in the sun, I wondered vaguely, if Tom would marry and give me some grandchildren.

After Prue's wedding, I'd expected Trevor's thoughts to turn to marriage, but it hadn't happened. I wondered if his deformity had held him back. His hand wasn't all that bad, but it made him very self-conscious. He behaved quite differently around his mates, with not a care in the world, but with women, he was intensely shy.

On this particular day by the sea, Jo lay sprawled beneath a canvas tent made by Rod, out of two modified deck chairs, to protect her from the sun. She was expecting twins! She was the only one of us who didn't go home brown as a berry from that memorable day.

I took Jo to the Spa for her promised massage and she spent a day relaxing and being pampered. I knew that when the twins arrived, she wouldn't have a moment to herself. It was the least I could do for her. Jo had always done so much for me. She and Rod still picked me up for church most Sundays, and I often thought what a handicap it was, me not to have learned to drive. It was an imposition on others too, perhaps I could take up lessons again when Tom was settled at Uni? I had started to pray for Tom's future, his safety and my strength to let him go, without him seeing that I minded so much. Before this impending separation, I admit I had just used the Church as a social club and never really believed in its precepts. But now I needed help. Tom's imminent move, was a big break for me. He was going to a new exciting life, but I was going to be left in the old one, now, quite alone.

What a 'Sadster' I was! But Tom was all I had left to remind me of Terry. Of course, I would still see him, from time to time. He would still be my son, but at a distance from now on, not sharing our home. Now I understood what the phrase 'Empty nest syndrome' meant.

What I didn't allow for though, was that where ever Tom went, Snuffles went too!

Top results enabled Tom to have a completely free choice of colleges and courses. He plumbed for the foundation course of 'Animal Management' at Chester. It was really a foregone conclusion.

As Snuffles couldn't be accommodated in the student's hostel, or at any of the private digs attached to the university, Tom got a special dispensation to live at home with my Mum, and bus in to college every day.

It was a brilliant arrangement and everyone was happy.

I struggled not to be selfish. I let a few tears out in front of my ever supportive Jo, and braced myself for the new life. I could do a course. I could look for a job. But from the money point of view, I didn't need one and most of what I could earn, with my limited qualifications, would go back to the government in tax

I went back to the gym on a daily basis working up my endorphins to dispel the impending gloom, I also threw myself into voluntary work at the Church, helping with clubs for every age group, from the nursery for hard pressed mums, to twilight clubs for those on walking frames. I baby sat regularly for Jo, and when her twins, Dylan and Christie were born 4 weeks early by caesarean section, I looked after Meg, taking her back and forth to kindergarten in the mornings, and making her lunch and tea, while she played happily round my feet, till Rod got back from the evening hospital visit to see Jo and the babes. It reminded me of being back at Kathy's with ?...for a moment I couldn't remember their names! Ah yes! Jamie and Lois. All the stress of Tom's leaving was having more of an effect on me than I'd realised After two weeks, Jo was allowed to bring them home. They were dear little chicks, un-identical boys. Dylan and Christie! Poor little Meg had wanted a sister, but she patted the boys gently and sung nursery rhymes to them, **when** she remembered, as she was only three.

That evening Tom phoned, full of the Joys of Spring. He loved the course, and had made several friends, most of them girls.

"Oh, Tom, what brill, news," I said, "I'm so pleased it's turning out so well for you. I love you!"

"I love you too, Mum. Nan sends her love, so does Snuffles."

"Bye then." he added and hung up.

Suddenly, the realisation that he had gone for good, hit me. I lay down on my bed and had a good cry.

Next morning, I thought of checking my computer for mail. Very few of my friends used emailing, so I often forgot to check, but I might check out the dating site, as well, It had been a while and maybe a flush of new men had signed up.

This time I thought I would try choosing, rather than be selected by another undesirable!

I looked through the list of men in my chosen category, 30-45 years old and living near. There were a few likely lads, but only one caught my eye.

His name was Edward, aka Gus. He was so handsome. Clean shaven, with thick wavy hair and strong cheek bones and that feature which always appealed to me, a cleft chin! He also lived within easy striking distance.

I went down to make my usual cup of coffee, to collect my thoughts, before emailing him.

'Things were very different for me now.' I thought, 'Tom was off hand. Settled and happy, Of course he'd be home for vacations, but eventually he would make his own life properly. May be settle for good in Cheshire, or travel. The world would open up for him. He might even decide to live abroad. I certainly didn't want him worrying about his old mum, alone at home.' "Well, I'm not old yet" I added, aloud, 'God,' I thought

'I've even started to talk to myself I must get a grip.' so I went back upstairs with my coffee, to contact Gus.

He replied by return.

"Clarice, thank you for your email. I've looked at your profile and I think it fits what I'm looking for. And you look lovely in the photo. If you want to start a conversation with me it would make me very happy."

"Yes" I replied I'd like that very much. You look like my kind of guy."

Nothing more, so I went for a walk in the still warm September sunshine. No Snuffles to pull me along! But my step was quite light as I walked to the park, being a bit unsure of going to the field that I usually tramped with Snuffles. It was probably safe, but one could never be quite sure. Snuffles had been my insurance policy.

When I got home for lunch I checked the computer. Nothing, so I went over to Jo's for the afternoon to see those adorable babies. Meg climbed straight up on my knee for her favourite story and the afternoon sped by.

Each day for a week, I checked my PC for an email from Gus. I suppose I could contact him again, but I didn't want to look needy. Instead I divided my time between helping Jo, keeping fit at the gym, helping at the Church. I looked for Lynne each time I went to the gym to see how dates were going, but she was never there. Perhaps she had met her love of a life-time! More likely she'd given up exercising. People came and went, their fads changing with their moods. Maybe her membership had run out and she couldn't afford to rejoin.

Then on the following Sunday evening, after a special service with a visiting preacher, I got home, feeling tired and drawn. The sermon had been dull and afterwards, I felt down and depressed instead of uplifted. I thought that I would check for emails, just once more before getting ready for bed. There it was in bright red type- 'You have a message from Gus!'

It read "Sorry I have been off line for so long. Had to go up to Surrey on business. Hope you didn't think I'd forgotten you! How are you Clarice. I'll be online all evening if you want to chat."

I had tried that stupid online chatting before. Putting in a little message, then waiting what seemed like hours, before a short typed answer came back. It was so irritating, and in between you suspected that your contact was probably chatting to other people on line simultaneously.

I typed back, "I'd rather you phoned me and we can chat properly, My number is ......"

The phone rang immediately.

"Hi Clarice!" he said "Good to talk to you. I was a bit nervous about asking for your phone number, so early on! How are you? Tell me all about yourself."

(That was a first! Men usually deluged you with talk about themselves!)

"Well!" I said "It's been a very long time since you wrote that first message saying you wanted to get to know me, or whatever. Then nothing! What's been happening? Where have you been? I'd almost given up on you?"

"Oh please, Clarice, never do that." He said "You sound so lovely. It's great to hear your voice. It fits in with your photo exactly." "Well tell me what kept you," I laughed. "What have you been up to? Do you work away?"

"No, not usually." He replied, "At the moment I'm staying with my mother, in Essex. Quite near you, I think, if I read your profile right? I have to travel down to Epsom quite frequently, at the moment, and sometimes I have to stay for a week or two, but that's been getting less recently."

"So what do you do?" I persisted.

"I'm a soldier." he said, "Well, I was, but I've finished my last tour of duty. Not quite sure what I want to do yet, but I've got a few ideas."

"What about you?" he asked.

"I'm just a boring old house wife. I do bits of charity work and help a friend out. But I'm really not that interesting," I replied.

"Looking like that, Clarice, you could never be boring! Could you send me some colour photos of you?" he asked, "It's hard to see your full beauty in black and white!"

"Are you taking the Mick? I said

"No, what do you mean?" he asked

"That's not a chat line I've heard before, it sounds weird. And I don't regard myself as beautiful."

"No of cause you wouldn't. Beauty is only in the eye of the beholder!"

"Ok then, When to you want to meet up and behold me?" I giggled.

"It's difficult at the moment", Gus said "I am tied into this ongoing thing, related to soldiering for at least another six or so weeks. I can't make any definite arrangements till it's over."

"What is it, a course or something?" I asked searching my mind for possibilities.

"Sort of" he said. "Look ," he continued, "Please send me loads of pictures of yourself, to keep me going, and, if you like, I'll send you a better photo of me. Then when we do meet, we'll recognise each other! How's that for a bargain? I'll email you my mum's address and give you my mobile number and we can stay in touch."

So that's what we did.

I waited for his photo to arrive in the post, hoping to see a photo of him standing to attention, in full army uniform. The photo did arrive, but it was a picture of him in civvies; Just his head and shoulders. But I didn't mind. Those piercing blue eyes made my heart race.

Over the weeks till we met, I found out quite a lot about Gus.

He had wanted to be a soldier all his life. He joined the CCF at school and loved the outward bound life. From thirteen, he went on exercises and loved the camping out and the night exercises. He even loved keeping his uniform clean and pressed, not letting his mum help. His favourite thing, he said was shining his boots!

'Well,' I thought, "those skills might come in useful in the future? Who knows!'

Apparently his father had died of a stroke before he enrolled as a regular soldier. He said it was a burst 'berry' or something in his head? And he had felt a bit guilty at leaving his mother on her own, but she had been very good about it. She had always known that he would join up at the first opportunity.

We talked about everything.Sometimes he was so busy he could only text, but from the rather shaky beginning he became an excellent communicator.

As well as our phone chats and endless texting, I couldn't wait to meet him in the flesh, so in the mean time, I developed my own special way of making him real to me.

Every morning, I had a conversation with his photo, which I'd had framed.

Gus sat on my dressing table, while I told him all the things we were going to do. Picnics in the woods, race each other round Snuffles' favourite field.

Barbeques every weekend that we were home, in the summer.

He could take over the cooking and maybe the sausages wouldn't get as burnt as they usually did! We could go to dancing classes, I had always wanted to dance but Terry wasn't keen. We might even go up to Queensway and take Jo skating, if Rod agreed to do the honours with the babies? I'd always wanted to learn to skate properly since that one and

only time Jo and I had gone together, before we had the flat. At least this time, if I slipped, Gus could hold me up. Also, if he had a car, and I presumed he had, he could drive me up to see Tom at Uni, and when we got really together (and I had a strong sense that we would) I could take him to meet my Mum and the family in Chester.

One morning my mind took flight, literally. What if, when his new job was settled, and his holidays were agreed, I could see if my flying phobia really had been cured by the dear Dr Baverstock. Then we could plan trips a broad.

Not to Barbados of course, but maybe the Maldives!? We could snorkel together and watch the golden Angel fish in their own habitat.

Chapter 14

I was so excited. Gus was coming to visit me. He had chatted endlessly on the phone to me, since getting back from his commitment in Surrey. He had told his mum all about me and apparently, she was almost as thrilled as he was!

We had exchanged so much about each other that I felt I knew him through and through. All his likes and dislikes, all his weird little habits. What food and drink he liked. Which television programs he watched. How he'd always wished he'd had a brother or sister to share his childhood with. About his pals at home when he was a kid, and then about his mates in the Army. How they all stuck together and it was like one big happy family, everyone looking out for each other. He told me that he had come to believe in God, while on active service. The lads always came together on a Sunday to listen to the Army chaplain's prayers. Most of them liked to feel that someone up there was looking after them, and Gus thought he could feel God's hand on his shoulder during the most terrifying times. "It was all blood and guts," he said "What held us together, was our community spirit. On active service, I found all the brothers I'd ever wanted."

I was watching out for him from the front room window. When his car drew up by the house, I could hardly contain get my breath and my heart was racing.

He wound the car window up, and I waited for him to jump out and race up the garden path into my arms.

But despite all our emails and texts and long phone calls late into the night, there was one thing that he had omitted to tell me! Something that I would never have imagined in a million years. As he struggled out of the car, I could see that his right arm was missing! His jacket sleeve hung empty, its cuff stuffed into his jacket pocket. I went cold and shivered. He would never be able to hug me! All those cuddles I'd imagined, were stopped in their tracks. Those sexy clinches, that I had lain in bed dreaming about, were never going to happen. I reached up towards him, with a wide smile covering my shock. I kissed him on the cheek.

"Hello darling" I said "it's wonderful to meet you at last."

"And you" he said, "You're even more beautiful in real life. Your photo's don't do you justice."

He could see that I didn't know what else to say. "Sorry about the arm" he said. "I should have told you." I nodded with a little 'it's ok' expression covering my true heart sink feelings. I hoped it was convincing. He walked along the path behind me. He had a slightly hesitant gait, but smiled broadly as he came into the hall. What a cosy little place you've got here. I showed him into the living room and sat down on the sofa and rested back.

"I'll go and make the tea". I said, rather too brightly. This first meeting was nothing like I had planned, or how I had hoped it would be. I couldn't explain my mixed bag of feelings even to myself. All his chat on the phone seemed to have dried up. He may have come to terms with the loss of his arm, the original shock having eased over the months, but my shock was indescribably raw. I had always prided myself with being able to come out with something... some comforting words, or showed genuine grief in my eyes for a very sick or bereaved patient when I did reception work at Willow Green, But now I was speechless.

Gus was right, he should have told me.

I went in with the tea tray, and some flap jacks I'd made that morning. One bit of information garnered from the late evening phone conversations was that he had a very sweet tooth.

As soon as I'd poured the tea, he said "Look, Clarice, I haven't been quite straight with you."

"No, I said you haven't. Why didn't you tell me about your arm?"

"I couldn't I knew you would never want to get to know me." He watched me carefully with those wonderful eyes. "Am I right, Clarice?" I thought 'Yes, quite right' I couldn't have dealt with it if I had known before hand, but so as not to hurt him, I said "Never mind, it doesn't matter now. You're here, that's all that matters! It must be terrible for you, I can't begin to think how you manage. How you've been able to get over it. Well, I suppose you haven't. Not really. Those sort of things take years don't they? I mean kids manage, but it must be much harder when you're older." I was wittering on with anxiety, so he gently interrupted me,

"I don't mean about my arm. I knew if I told you my story you wouldn't give me a chance. But when I saw your photo on the dating site, I fell in love with you right away. I wanted to meet you face to face, before you made up your mind about me. The reason I couldn't come and see you before, was because I've had to go for long sessions of rehab. And limb fittings at the army rehab centre in Epsom I told myself that I didn't have time to explain to you, but really I've been too cowardly. I've been wondering over and over, how I would ever be able to tell you." I frowned completely puzzled by what he was saying. 'What limb fittings?' I thought, he isn't wearing a false arm, his sleeve is empty.'

"Tell me what?" I asked. In answer, he pulled up his trouser legs to show me his peg legs. Gus was a triple amputee!

He had joined the Army as a cadet at sixteen. At eighteen he was posted to Germany and from there sent over to the troubles in Ireland. From then on his life was ruled by explosions screams, clouds of dust and gunfire.

After a spell in Iraq he was sent to Afghanistan. On the day he was blown up, he was on his way to take supplies to an outlying village in the Sangin region of Helmand province. That's where his army career ended, tripping a previously unidentified IED (improvised explosive device), hidden in the thick undergrowth. When the Medics brought him back to base camp on the stretcher, they thought he was dead. For a long time afterwards, having had endless unsuccessful surgery, to try and save his shredded arm, he had wished that he **had** died at the time of the explosion. His lower legs had been smashed by the blast, so the field surgeons only had to tidy up what was left of them. They told him that he was very lucky to only need below knee amputations.

Gus explained that this was the reason he'd been so cagey about the weeks he'd spent away, not being able to contact me. He had been going for rehabilitation at Headley Court, in Surrey, where they had state-of-the-art limb fitting. it was widely acknowledged that double or triple amputee soldiers with prosthetic limbs 'had become one of the enduring images of the present conflicts' It said so on the Headley Court leaflet that he brought to show me. I guess in previous wars, soldiers died when their limbs were blown off. What price progress?

At Headley Court, there were 'bionic hands' and micro-chipped legs. Hydrotherapy pools, specialised Physiotherapy, and gyms with all the latest hi- tech equipment.

I couldn't read any further, or take any more in.

"Your tea must be cold by now. I'll go and put the kettle on again." I said to him

In the kitchen, I thought 'Where do we go from here?' I would need a life-time to adjust to this situation. To this man!

When I returned with more tea, he smiled at me with his piercing blue eyes surrounded by crinkly laugh lines. It was incredible that a human being could bear so much, endure such damage and still be smiling. He was a brave, brave man. But was I a brave enough woman to take him on?

He told me he had avoided any head injury, and so his perfect vision had remained intact. Without, that he wouldn't have been able to appreciate me. "Clarice," he said "If I couldn't see you now, I would have missed seeing the best thing of my entire my life. You are beautiful!" he was good at flattery, making it sound sincere, but he was so very handsome himself that I wondered, had he been able-bodied, whether he would have given me a second glance.

I sat beside him on the sofa while we had our second cup of tea. He was charming. I knew a lot about him. In fact, he had told me everything about himself over the weeks before we finally met, except the very things that were now holding us back, stopping us losing ourselves in each other's passionate embrace.

"Where do we go from here?" he asked mirroring my thoughts. "I love you already," he said

"And I thought I loved you, but you knew the whole truth and I didn't." I said with a thin smile.

"OK. "he said. "Point taken. Mother told me this would happen. She warned me to be more open about things before you saw me, but I was frightened of your reaction. She was right."

'How could a man, this brave be afraid, of me' I wondered.

"Tell you what! Would you like to go out next weekend? We could go to the zoo!"

And that's how it started. We became firm friends. We went to all sorts of places in London, galleries, museums, the South Bank. He came to the Church. He met Jo and her family. Wherever we went he was justly hailed as a hero. My hero! I joined the British Legion with him and we helped with fund raising events. He talked to Women's groups about the war, and was asked to speak at the Rotary club.

I insisted that he continued to live with his mum, but sometimes he stayed over at mine. We had a lot of fun together, and I started to get used to having him around. But it took me a long time to get used to his appearance even fully clothed, and much, much longer to see him naked.

Chapter 15

In every other way Gus was the perfect man. He was charming and romantic, loved by everyone. My friends, Mum and all the family, all liked him and thought he was amazing. Tom admired him and Snuffles would have licked him all over if he could. As things were, the dog had to make do with just Gus's face; and so did I.

Well… Gus would have liked a lot more intimacy, but for me the step from loving friendship to lover was a giant leap. He wanted me badly, I knew how he felt, and I did love the man. I loved his handsome face, his heart, and spirit, his kindness and love for me and mine, but no matter how I tried to get over it, I could not overcome the revulsion I felt when I thought about his injuries, those injuries he had sustained, while fighting so selflessly for his country. I knew this made me to appear quite the opposite to him; a selfish and hard-hearted bitch. I could have wept for the situation. We continued as sister and brother and eventually I plucked up courage to ask him if I could see what remained of his legs. Even though I knew it would be bad, the revelation shocked me! The stumps of Gus' legs reminded me of enormous versions of Trevor's deformed fingers, which had haunted me, since I was a girl. It was one thing to have these feelings about a little brother, but this beautiful broken man was my potential lover. I remembered how I had tried hard to avoid looking at little Trev's fingers. The end of Gus's left stump looked a bit similar, like a shrivelled sausage. The skin was drawn in and twisted, as if to stop the minced up sausage meat it contained, from escaping. The right stump was finished off better. He told me that the stumps often became sore from rubbing on their prosthetic sockets, because they weren't a perfect fit. The sockets were lined with a soft inner cuff, but blisters still formed and sometimes these broke down into ulcers. I said how sorry I was, speaking to him softly and caringly, which was how I felt for Gus the patient, but inside I was trying to beat down the rising nausea at the thought of ulcers on the ends of these stumps. The sight of them healed was bad enough. I tried to appear normal while looking at them, but inside I was trembling, and after a few moments, I had to look away from the stunted limbs and fix my gaze on Gus's face.

"How do you manage them, when they get sore?" I asked.

"Well, Mum offered to dress them, for me herself, but I thought it would be too much for her, so we always ask the District Nurse to come in."

"Are they terribly painful?" I asked. He nodded.

I could have cried for him.

One Saturday we walked for far too long, and when we got back Gus looked drained. That evening he went up to bed early. Next morning, at breakfast, he told me that his left stump had broken down and he was going to call the District Nurse out to dress it. When she arrived I went out to the kitchen to make her a cup of tea, and then, when I came back into the living room I put it down on the table for her and made myself watch her clean the wound. She smiled, seeing I was interested and started to show me how to do the dressing.

"You could do it next time, if you like, Clarice," she said, I'll be here to help you and check that you aren't having any problems with it. Then after that, you can take over. It'll be one less customer on my list!" She grinned at Gus. We all smiled and when she had finished and thrown all the waste cotton wool and gauze into the bin, I showed her out.

"I couldn't!" I whispered "I'm so sorry."

Gus said "That's OK. When my Mum first saw them, she said she decided that she couldn't bear to dress them either."

My thoughts kept flipping between 'I didn't sign up for this,' and 'You poor darling, I wish I could do something to ease your pain.'

Gus was all too aware of my dilemma. He could still **feel** his legs and only knew they were gone when he looked. Sometimes his toes or feet would ache, or neuralgic phantom limb pains would shoot though his legs, but there was nothing I could do. No where for me to apply a soothing balm. I could neither see nor feel his lost limbs. Nor could I see a way out of our predicament.

He did still stay with me sometimes at weekends, but less and less frequently. Our longed for relationship was failing to improve, and I knew it was my fault. I had made him sleep in the spare bedroom from the outset. I know this hurt his feelings and was terribly hard for him. He was a red blooded young man in his prime, five years younger than me. Because of my fear of his body, I tried to make sure he never felt aroused by me. I never let him fondle me or kiss me properly. I was careful not to wear revealing clothes, though I didn't have many of those anyway, and I always came down to breakfast fully dressed.

I think we both thought that the end was in sight.

The break through came when I caught 'flu. I had a fever and ached all over, feeling too ill to even move from my bed. Gus stayed at my house and brought me drinks and aspirin, and was generally as kind and thoughtful as he could be.

By the third day I felt a bit better, so in the evening, after he'd had tea he came up and lay on my bed to read me snippets from the 'Mail.' I must have dozed off, because when I awoke it was pitch black outside. I closed my eyes again and felt a hand gently stroking my shoulder. I moved towards the hand and felt his lips on mine, and then the gentle probing into my soft moist nether regions. It was our first coming together. It was wonderful. I realised afterwards, that now, all I ever had to do was **feel** the sensation, without sight or sound or thought. My concentration on one primary, compelling sensation alone, would cut out all other invading thoughts, and would allow that delicious sensation to grow and grow, to such proportions, that the climax would always be earth shattering! At last Heaven was ours!

I came down to breakfast the next day, and Gus was all smiles. He held my hand over the boiled eggs and said"I was right Clarice, we were made for each other! I'll never let you go."

I squeezed his hand in agreement. He was my man and I never **wanted** him to let me go!

Gus had been promised various desk jobs by the Army, after he recovered, but with the cut backs, they never came to anything.

He set up a web site for injured ex-soldiers, which gave them important information, but also lent them his personal support and advice. Nobody could have known more than he, what a struggle it could be to get back to normal life after leaving the army, even without a disability. To loose the camaraderie, and the security of the army which provided your every daily need, and to also leave behind the excitement and intensity of working as a close knit team, was unbelievably hard.

He also knew that a lot of families found it hard to deal with their ex-soldier husband or father. A man who had lived for years on the edge of the battlefield with the sounds of sirens, gunfire, bomb blasts and screams of the dying. Seeing his fellow soldiers mangled and killed and innocent women and children injured and left homeless, was always going to find it difficult to settle down to permanent home life in the UK, having previously only been home for leave. Army leave starts with the hype of reunion with loved ones, laughing and crying with extremes of emotion, followed by a short interlude of relative happiness, when everyone is on their best behaviour, followed by an emotional send off, with flags and brass bands, as the soldier leaves for his next field of action. After leaving the Army, a soldier's life, previously lived on constant adrenaline rushes, can easily become depressing, and threaded through with a sense of loss; Both loss of his comrades and of the exciting life that bound them together.

So Gus's web site was a God send to others veterans, some injured like himself, and some feeling desperate. It also linked him up with some of his old buddies, and he made hundreds of new friends and contacts as well. The site and his charity work, overflowed his days.

He wanted to move in with me, but though most of the obstacles had now dissolved, I still didn't like the idea of him moving into Terry's old home; the home where we had brought up Tom together. There were too many memories.

Gus had quite a good Army pension and I was relatively well off, with the combination of investments from the Lottery win and Terry's life insurance, so money was not a problem. Eventually after several weeks of house hunting we came upon a little cottage on the edge of Epping Forest, within easy reach of his mum. Though to me, who had been tied to Public transport, since Terry's death, anywhere could be described as 'within easy reach', now that Gus drove me everywhere. His car had been specially adapted for him, though he could manage the pedals they were a bit higher than usual.

The thing he missed most, in every situation, was his right hand.

We bought 'Violet cottage' on the edge of Epping Forest. We chose that name because on the day we moved in we discovered that the previous owners had left a beautiful African violet on the kitchen window sill. It was deep purple velvet with juicy stems and succulent leaves. Gus thought this was an omen of our future life together. There was no upstairs to make things easier for Gus, so I suppose, strictly speaking it was a bungalow, but it was so pretty, we always thought of it as our cottage. There were masses of sweet smelling pink and gold honeysuckle growing round the front door; it was this and the pretty little garden at the back that persuaded us both, that it was our dream home.

And guess who would be doing the gardening now!

All expectations of the good life came true.

Our circle of friends grew to include the local villagers, Gus's ex-solder mates, friends we had made through St Winifred's, and of course, Jo and family.

Gus was my personal hero, but I didn't mind sharing him with all his fans. We were ideally happy.

Gus was always in seventh heaven when Jo and Rod brought their children round to see us. Meg, at three, was becoming a sweet little girl and was my favourite, but I noticed Gus was enamoured by the Christie and Dylan, the bouncing twins. He looked at me shyly whenever they came over and I sensed that he would love to have a child of his own. Well, I was pushing forty and who could say if my eggs were good to go? Probably with the help of IVF it would have been possible, but whatever else I could do, I knew I would not be able to deal with Gus and a new baby...worse a toddler! That would indeed be a step too far.

We never discussed the matter, but instead we chose a sweet moggie from the cat refuge. Actually, 'No', she chose us, as Snuffles had chosen Tom and me years before. Primrose, a fluffy tabby, sat in front of our log fire and completed the idyll.

And then everything changed!

It all began one night when I was woken by a single scream, high pitched and inhuman! I sat bolt upright in bed. After a moment, I turned towards Gus to see what he made of it, but he was still fast asleep, thought sweating profusely. I pulled the duvet off him towards my side, and lay back. Perhaps it was a fox? Foxes let out strange screeching barks, didn't they? I sank back into my dream.

Several nights later, it happened again. This time I knew it wasn't a fox. It was coming from the heroic ex-soldier who lay beside me. In his dreams, he was back on the battlefield. Tears were streaming down his taut, white features; then he started shaking and sobbing like a frightened child. He didn't appear to wake up until the end of whatever terror he was reliving, but when he did open his eyes, he turned away from me to stare at the blank wall.

The night terrors became more and more frequent. There was no pattern to them. Sometimes, several nights would pass without any disturbance. We would make love and afterwards, Gus would sleep like a baby. Time and again I was given false hope, and thought that it was a passing phase. When the terrors did return they were worse than ever.

I tried to talk to Gus about them. At first he was in denial and refused to listen to me or discuss his feelings at all. I wondered if perhaps he didn't remember them in the morning. Maybe he was just working through them in a dreamlike state.

Then he started to get tetchy during the day. He would pick rows with me over the smallest nothing. Everything had to be done perfectly, and **his** way. Gradually his irritability got worse and he started shouting at me for the least thing. His behaviour was coming between us and I was afraid to ask people round any more. He was in total denial, and said there was nothing wrong with him. I didn't know what to do. I'd heard my parents talk about 'shell shock' in the WW1 and read about 'Gulf war syndrome' Some said it was due to all the jabs the soldiers were made to have that might have damaged their immune system, but what about Afghanistan. Did soldiers get a syndrome from there? Gus didn't talk to me at all about his time in Helmand province, but I sometimes overheard him talk to the other guys who had been out there with him.

The crunch came Sunday morning. He hit me. Afterwards, he was mortified. It was that incident that seemed to bring him to his senses. He broke down and his whole body shuddered with sobs. Through the anguish, he began to tell me about the Hell he had gone through, and it was clear that that same

Hell was still entrenched deep down in his mind. He told me about the sounds; the shrill commands, the bomb blasts, the anguished screams of the injured, the endless rattle of gunfire. He told me about the sights; the blood gushing from the gaping wounds of his fellow soldiers, local women clutching broken children to their breasts, body parts hanging from branches. He told me about the smells; the all-pervading smoke of burning buildings, the putrefaction of gangrenous wounds, the stench of cholera victims lying in their own shit. His brain could no longer keep under lock and key the sheer awfulness of what he had experienced, and was making him relive it night after night. Finally the dam had burst. His terrified outpourings made him shudder.

Gus thought he was losing his mind.

First thing, Monday morning I phoned for an appointment with my new GP, to whom my past was a closed book.

10am on a Wednesday morning found me in Dr Evans surgery, and by 10.05 I was howling into the wad of tissues she passed me. Having noticed my black eye and listened to the stammered account of my relationship problems, she picked up on the fact that Gus was suffering from Post Traumatic Shock Disorder. Apparently, the fact was, that what had seemed to me the most terrible thing in the world, the loss of three limbs, had actually delayed the appearance of something much worse, the PTSD.

Dr Evans explained to me that Gus had spent so much energy and concentration on learning to overcome his physical disabilities, that the trauma to his mind had been buried. It wasn't till he had understood the suffering of his fellow soldiers, who hadn't been applauded as heroes, and talked to the widows and families of soldiers who hadn't returned, that his guilt as a survivor, albeit, a very damaged one, began to hit home and allow his psychological hurt to surface.

She recommended, as she noted my black eye, that he return to stay at his Mother's and seek help from a Military psychiatrist. Meanwhile she prescribed me some Valium, ½

-1 tablet prn. There were only 14 in the box when I got them from the Chemist and as I thought I wouldn't need them, when I got home I put them at the back of the drawer in my bedside cabinet.

On the way home in the taxi, I made three decisions. Gus would stay with me, he would make an appointment with the Army shrink, and meanwhile I would explain the problem to dear old Dr Baverstock and see if he could come up with a cure.

Chapter 16

Gus didn't need to be persuaded to contact the defences Medical Rehab Centre at Headley Court. He was a broken man. After his catharsis, I wasn't worried that he would attack me again.

Headley court had done so much for his physical injuries, but he was nervous about going back for psychological help. The other guys he'd met on line with mental problems had found psyche aid hard to access, mainly because of cutbacks and a shortage of Psychologists trained

to deal with PTSD. None the less he contacted them as soon as he could get himself together. He knew how much was at stake. Our relationship and home together were his main support, if he lost them he thought he would be back to square one, and much as he and his mother loved each other, the strain would have been overwhelming for both of them.

An appointment was not forthcoming. They would do the best they could to get him an early assessment interview, but then the wait for treatment was a matter of months, because so many traumatised soldiers needed help.

When this sunk in, it wasn't hard to persuade Gus to visit my trusty old friend, Dr Baverstock, who had helped me through so many of difficulties in my life. I was sure he would be able to do something to ease the night terrors, even if he couldn't get right to the bottom of the problem.

Gus only made one stipulation, and that was, that I would stay with him during all the discussions and treatments. Of course I agreed and this was a plus, as I certainly would not have been allowed to be present at any kind of therapy offered by the Military.

Gus was frightened by his violent reaction to his nightmares, attacking the one person he loved more than anyone on earth, but he was even more

scared of what hypnosis might bring out from him. After all, he had been trained as a killing machine.

We went to the first consultation, and Dr Baverstock met us at the door with his usual old world charm. I noticed that despite first meeting him some years before, he hadn't appeared to have aged.

"Ah, Clarice," he said "How lovely to see you again, my dear. And this must be Gus." He held out his hand to Gus and as he took it, the Doctor gripped it firmly and raised it, quite quickly, high into the air, almost, as if to kiss it.

As the two men's hands parted, and dropped to their sides, I could see that a change had come over Gus. The nervousness that he had shown as we walked up the path to meet the hypnotist, had left him. I got the feeling that the magic had already begun.

We were led into the inner sanctum, where Gus took the seat opposite the Doctor, looking more relaxed than I'd seen him in months. I sat beside Gus.

I had told Dr B the essence of the problem, on the phone, when we made the appointment, but now I kept silent.

"Now Gus," Dr B said quietly "tell me a little about what has brought you here to see me today."

In the healing atmosphere of this gentle man's consulting room, Gus was able to explain how he had struggled to recover from his very severe injuries, while trying to help his fellow veterans. As he spoke, I watched the doctor mirror Gus's gestures and expressions with great empathy. When Gus began to stumble over his words, the doctor took over from him …

"You are a hero, my son!" he said "I am deeply honoured to meet such a brave man. Our country, and indeed the whole world, needs more strong hearted, honourable young men like you." He leant forward and took Gus's left hand in his and instead of patting it, as I one pats someone on the shoulder, he lifted it up determinedly into the air, while looking straight into Gus's eyes. As he let go, I could see Gus had fallen into a deep trance. Under hypnosis, he asked Gus about conditions at the front, never searching too deeply, and keeping things calm, he told Gus to answer his questions with just a nod or shake of the head.

By the end of the session, using simple head movements, Gus revealed some of the most terrifying ordeals he had endured. He shed some tears and showed by his facial expression that he was re-viewing the ordeals without re-experiencing them, as he did during his night terrors.

After he was restored to full awareness, the doctor said

"Gus, you are even braver than I could have imagined. Next time, while you are in a very relaxed state, I am going to use a treatment called 'Eye Movement Desensitisation and Reprocessing' All the time you will stay in a light hypnotic trance, so that you will feel quite at peace. I am going to ask you to bring up the memory of each upsetting event and we will establish a link between your consciousness and the sites where these memories are stored. Afterwards you will retain the memories but they will cease to trouble you or be intrusive. They will stop jumping out to bite you." Gus nodded. The doctor continued "You are not alone in your feelings of survivor guilt you know." Again Gus nodded "It can be caused in many ways," he continued "in all situations where a lot of people die, like plane crashes for instance, where only a few 'lucky' ones survive. You **are** lucky to be alive, because you have Clarice to love. She is a dear girl, and I know she loves you very much too. Go home and relax together over a bottle of wine. Sleep tonight will be very much easier than of late. Remember the dreams will be there in your head but you will know, in your heart, that over the next few sessions, you **will** be cured."

He shook hands with both of us again, but this time, I noticed that he shared an ordinary man-to-man handshake with Gus.

"What an extraordinary fellow!" said Gus as we walked to the car.

I **will** follow up with the Army Psyche, when the appointment comes through, but I do think that your Dr Baverstock knows what he's doing, and I feel really safe with him."

"I hope it works." I said, holding Gus's arm.

'Yes' I thought 'Because one more black eye and I'm out'

But my lips were firmly set into a hopeful smile. Dr Baverstock always seemed to lighten my heart, even, it seemed, if I wasn't the patient!

That night I took my first valium.

Since the first hypnotic session, Gus's moods had stabilised. He was still very restless at night, tossing and turning, grabbing the duvet and then pushing it off, talking excitedly in his sleep. He was calmer than before and I stopped feeling in danger from his previously unexplained outbursts. On the nights we made love, when some of his excess energy was used up, he slept more calmly. I was quietly hopeful.

The protocol was the same each time.

Dr Baverstock came to the door to welcome us, smiling at me, and giving Gus, what I took to be a handshake of induction into a hypnotic trance. What else could it be?

Since our first visit, I'd been puzzling over where I'd seen that trick before, and then I remembered. It was used as a gimmick on a TV show about stage hypnosis. Somehow it looked even more weird, taking place in somebody's front hall, but Gus seemed to accept it as a natural greeting!

Dr B explained what they were going to do in this and all the following sessions. He and Gus would work together in what he described as a 'therapeutic partnership.'

The doctor told Gus how the EMDR treatment the was going to work. Gus listened intently, though his eyes were slightly glazed. I listened too and tried my hardest to remember what was said. I so hoped it would work, because we had nothing else to hang on to. Somehow I doubted that Gus, who was already looking somewhat dazed, would remember much about it afterwards. That's what I had found with hypnosis. You don't remember anything that was said in the session for a couple of days, then, out of the blue, ideas start to clarify, as if they are entirely your own. You wonder why you had never thought of those solutions before, it suddenly all seemed so simple.

I was thinking that if this EMDR did work, we could recommend it to other ex-service men with similar problems.

Dr Baverstock watched Gus intently as he started the explanation, it is complicated, but this is the gist of what I think he said.

"EMDR involves getting your eyes to move from left to right rapidly, closely following the path of my index finger. Each traumatic episode will be broken down into its sensory elements, with every set of eye movements. Each sensation, associated with each trauma will be brought to the surface and we will dispel it." I was beginning to lose the thread and decided to ask Dr B for an explanatory leaflet before we left.

"It's thought," he continued "That EMDR may replicate the rapid eye movements of the dreaming state. So, Gus, you will always be in a deeply hypnotic state while I ask you to think about one of those past traumatic episodes. When I raise my voice, I will ask you 'How bad is the smell?' This will be the signal for you to re-experience the smell part of the trauma as strongly as possible. This exhausts the system. Gus, do you understand what I'm telling you?" Gus nodded. All the time Dr B kept reassuring Gus that he would stay hypnotised throughout. He emphasised that deep mind traumas would only be addressed during hypnotic trance, so that Gus would never be upset by the procedure. We will work through sound and sight and touch as well as the smell of each trauma in turn, and even taste, if that is appropriate, till they are all neutralised and reprocessed into simple non-intrusive memories.

"Your eyes will always follow my finger and you will always follow my exact instructions. Is that OK with you, Gus?"

Again came the nod and murmured "Yes"

"Finally" said the doctor, "At the end of each session, before bringing you to full alertness, I will ask you about your hopes for the future."

The doctor smiled benignly and started to bring Gus out of trance.

'Well! mumbo-jumbo or what?' I thought ' but if it works, it works' It all sounded so muddled, partly, I think, because the doctor had hypnotised me, in the past and the sound of his voice, even when it wasn't directed at me, still made my thinking hazy.

At the end of the next session, having thought about it more clearly during the intervening week, I remembered to ask Dr Baverstock if he did have any handouts or explanatory leaflets on this type of treatment.

"I **will** get you some reading matter Clarice. But let's wait till our dear Gus is out of the wood. Is that alright with you, my dear?"

I think he thought I was going to try some of his techniques myself and possible muck up his efforts! Nothing was further from my mind, but I agreed, it would be better to wait. When 'Gus **was** out of the wood' he himself would be able to use material from the pamphlets to put on his website. This would definitely be the best way to spread the word to the many other war vets who were suffering from post traumatic shock.

The sessions continued weekly and then fortnightly for what seemed like a lifetime.

Gus always insisted that I accompany him. As he improved mentally, it seemed that the treatment was bringing Gus and I closer together. Towards the end of the course of treatment, he cancelled the assessment appointment at Headley Court, thinking that someone else with less resources, could make use of it.

At last Gus's symptoms had gone. He slept like a baby, and his life was as normal as it could ever be. He continued helping and advising other ex-servicemen who had been terribly traumatised, whether by physical wounds or mental experiences.

The EMDR leaflet, finally given to us by Dr B, which to me was his secret sign that Gus had the 'all clear', went up on the website, and with it Gus added links to sites for 'Emotional freedom therapy'(EFT) which Dr Baverstock had also shown him.

Tapping for good emotional health! And I thought I used to be the mad one!

Now we'd been free from all the recent angst, I wondered if I ought to start looking for a part-time job. Gus asked me not to, as I was literally his 'right-hand woman'. I went everywhere with him, to support him at the talks he gave, at meetings and reunions, and he, in turn, always drove me everywhere I wanted to go. We went up to see Tom in his final year at Chester Uni, to my Mum's…she had really come out of herself since Dad died, and to visit sister Prue, who, had, at last managed to produce a grand daughter for my Mum! Saskia was a bouncing ball of fun, eating everything in sight, nothing like Prue, in fact, she reminded me of myself as a child. I did hope she wouldn't have to go through as many ups and downs in life as me! But then we all have the good times and the bad, it's probably just how we look at things that makes us either bubbly or flat!

These days we were asked out to so many functions that it was quite a treat just to stay in and stroke Primrose by our log fire. While we were doing just this one evening, with our supper trays on our laps…Yes, Gus did have a sort of lap and had developed a very good sense of balance… He said it would be nice if one evening, we went out for a romantic evening, just the two of us.

"Would you like that Clarice? You've put up with so much from me. I'd really like to wine and dine you, as we should have done in the beginning."

"I'd love that," I said

"I know it all went wrong, in the beginning. I should have told you all about myself. But I didn't want to frighten you away before we even met. Then it all went pear-shaped."

"You've apologised before, darling," I said "There's absolutely no need to go over it all again. Now I know everything there is to know about my one-armed bandit, I love you more than ever!"

"And I love you too, Clarice. You are my darling heart." I knelt by his chair and he bent to kiss me. The glass of water slipped off his tray, and splashed all over us both! What was that I said about him having a good sense of balance?

Two weeks later, he took me out to dinner at a swish little restaurant in Epping, renowned for its good food. He had booked a table for two, in our own alcove, with a starched white cloth and candles.

Gus ordered Champagne. Then my eyes widened as he passed me a little blue card board box. Inside was a heart-shaped gold locket, studded with tiny rubies. I loved it! He walked round behind me to fasten the fine chain round my neck, and as he did he bent kiss me gently on the neck.

Life was such a mad rush with all the events we attended, that I hadn't noticed the date. February 14th, St Valentine's Day!

He kissed my neck again, and then he whispered in my ear, "Clarice, you are the best and dearest thing that has ever happened to me. I don't deserve you, but I love you. Will you be my Valentine?"

I was giggling by the time he sat down. The colour was rising up into my cheeks

"We're not seventeen, you know!" I said

"No, I know," he answered, "but when I was seventeen, I had no idea what romance was about. I thought it was stupid. Sloppy and sentimental stuff.

I was macho. Sex was the thing then...well, it still is." He laughed "But you have taught me how to love and allow myself to be loved. Those are priceless gifts you've given me." I was all smiles, wondering if I had a small enough photo of him and one of Tom, to put in the locket.

The rest of the evening passed blissfully in bubbles of champagne, I can't even remember the menu! In the cab going home we started to snog and once inside the front door, lust took over. Poor Primrose wondered what on earth was happening. In the bedroom we made passionate love, all the more delicious, because Gus had already perfected the art of giving ingenious one-handed pleasures, and of course, tongues were deeply involved. After love-making we slept the sleep of the dead.

Streaming sunshine and breezes blowing through the half open curtains woke us. The fresh forest air seemed to blow away any after effects from the champers. I sat bolt upright, in bed and said

"Gus, will you marry me?" His eyes were shining and even deeper blue than I remembered.

"Yes Clarice, I certainly will! All you need to do is name the day!"

We both giggled and hugged and rolled over in bed, and as the champagne must have still been lurking in our systems, we made love all over again.

Chapter 17

We decided on a June wedding.

I guess most people would have to plan years ahead for a marriage at this time of year, to book a grand hotel and all the extras. I'd heard that a wedding could cost as much as 20k, with insurance on top, in case someone changed their mind!

Anyway we were going to do it on the cheap, and it was going to be wonderful!

The first thing we did have to do was book the church. Of course we wanted St Winifred's although it wasn't our parish church. We lived outside the parish, so we made an appointment to see David, the new vicar. David said the church was available for the 14th and so was he, and there was nothing he would like more than to marry us, and he knew his whole congregation would feel the same when they found out. He was a lovely man. Gus and I had decided not to send out invitations, so we asked the vicar if he would announce our engagement and invite everyone to the wedding service and to the reception afterwards. We also asked if the reception could be held in the big hall behind the church and the Vicar was over the moon. Of course, he said, there would be a standard charge for the wedding and an extra one for use of the hall. Did we want a choir? and of course we would need an organist. The banns would have to be called for three Sundays running before the wedding as we didn't actually live in the parish bounds.

"Golly!" I said "there's so much more to do than I thought, already"

Both the men smiled and David said

"Just make sure you remember to get the marriage licence, Gus. You need to go to the Registrar's office, and get it at least a month before the wedding"

"OK Vicar, it'll be the first thing on my list. Thanks so much for sorting us out." Gus shook David's hand. "I don't think either of us thought getting married would be so complicated!" he said.

I smiled but kept quiet. They both knew I was a widow. I wasn't going to start bleating about how much easier it had been last time. A quick and easy ceremony, dragging a couple of willing bystanders, off the street to act as witnesses and tying the knot with Terry at the Registry office! That was my past. In it's own way, it was a beautiful memory of Terry and me. But it was my own beautiful memory, shut away in a private compartment in my mind, which no one could unlock.

My second marriage was going to be a confirmation of our life together, the life Gus and I had already built. But this time I was really going to blossom into being a bride, and enjoy every minute.

Gus put a general invitation to all his contacts on his website, saying all his war veterans were welcome, but he would like a reply by email to confirm numbers. Within a day he was showered by congratulations and acceptances. Twelve of the ex-soldiers offered to mount a guard of honour at the church door, for each of us, as we arrived singly and then afterwards, as we left as a married couple. I thought only Royalty had guards of honour, but being such a hero, Gus was treated like Royalty where ever we went. Several of the prospective guards, who were completely ambulant, offered to double as ushers. And a handful of guys who'd survived Afghanistan unscathed, (physically anyway) offered to club together and pay for a car to drive us away from the church to our honeymoon destination.

I couldn't believe how well it was working out, and how kind everyone was!

We were going to have printed orders of service, but not have left and right sides of the church for his and hers. We decided everyone would mix together, they were all our friends and it would be truly inclusive.

The one thing I was insistent about was having a proper C of E, prayer book order of service. I wanted to hear the words 'I, Edward Gustav Hewitt, take you Clarice Smith, to be my wedded wife, to have and to hold from this day forward…to love and to cherish till death us do part.' (how I wished I had a middle name!)

We took out the bit about sickness as we'd already been through that and the bit about richer or poorer, because unless the whole share market collapsed, we would always be solvent. At the 'exchange of rings I wanted to include 'love and **obey'** when I had to say my bit, but Gus wouldn't hear of it.

"Obey me!" he sounded aghast. "It's more likely that I ought to obey you!" So we left it out.

Of course we weren't going to be able to **exchange** rings either, because although Gus had a ring finger, he needed his left hand to be as free as possible, to do the work of two; plus, because his balance wasn't perfect he might totter and a ring could catch on something and injure his hand.

We chose the ring together. I wanted gold, to match the locket.

It was sent away to be engraved with C &G in a curly style.

Next on the agenda was my dress. I had really wanted papery silk with a silvery sheen, but Jo and I looked in all the magazines and could only come up with cream. I settled for a full length fitted dress scattered with tiny seed pearls. The headpiece was a pearl tiara in floaty lace; Obviously not enough to cover my face, but enough to flow with the design of the dress. As the assistant was helping me choose it in the wedding dress shop, I had a sudden flashback to my appearance on that celebrity program. Gus must have been in some war zone, thousands of miles away, when it was televised, so he knew nothing about it. In fact we knew nothing much at all about each other's past lives! I wondered if I could find my photos to show him ?

I chose cream roses for the bouquet intermingled with pink 'baby breath', The pink would be reflected in Meg's raspberry pink bridesmaid's dress. She would be my only attendant as the twins were too young and my little niece, just a baby.

Tom asked me if he could give me away!

"Not that I'll ever really give you away to anyone, I mean only do what Grandad would have done if he was still alive."

"Yes, Tom," I said "I do know what you mean."

I was so thrilled that Tom backed me over the wedding so wholeheartedly. It Must be difficult for any child to accept a step parent into the family, especially if their own mum or dad has died. I thought it might be easier for Tom, if his dad was still alive, to be visited. Then having a step dad would be just be an extra person in the family for him, not a replacement. But of course no one could ever replace Terry in Tom's eyes. Nor would I **ever** have replaced Terry if he hadn't died. We were wedded for life, 'till death do us part,' even though we hadn't had to say those words to the Registrar who married us.

Gus surprised me by asking Trevor to be his best man. Trevor was touched and accepted immediately. I think he started working on his speech there and then.

I was a bit surprised that Gus hadn't asked one of his own friends, but I suppose he thought it better 'keep it in the family.'

We wanted to make a special fuss of both our mothers, and they would be the only ones to sit on the correct side of the church for their child. Well, we weren't exactly children, but you know what I mean. His Mum on the right and mine on the left with Prue and co.

I went up to Chester and took Mum out to choose a dress for the occasion. In the end she decided on a dove grey and pink print, in silk with matching pink gloves and dark grey shoes. It sounds a bit dull but she looked so smart in the outfit that I came near to tears. I thought back over my childhood and all I could remember seeing her in was her greasy pinny, though she must been wearing something like a blouse and skirt underneath. I just could not picture it in my mind.

I wondered about their marriage. What had Dad been like when they got married, before drink got the better of him? I asked Mum to get out all the family photos, and there weren't many. Those were the days of box cameras, after Sepia and before digital. There was an old snap of them as a young couple, it was slightly blurred and hard to make out. They were both smiling, but then people always do in photos! Nothing is given away by expressions, after the camera operator says 'cheese'. Mum was thinner then than she had been all my young life, and now, with less worry, she'd become slimmer again and smarter. I wondered how Gus and I would be together after ten or twenty years of marriage. Would we still be happy in Violet Cottage? Would we still love each other as we did now, or would it all have worn a bit thin. Would we still make love, with or without Champagne .

Talking of photos, Tom said he and a mate from college would organise the photography, and would we like a DVD as well? "I'll think about it, Tom," I said "but if you could take the photos it would be brilliant." I gave him a hug "Thanks, darling." "Mum, the DVD would be no trouble, honestly" I didn't like to tell him we hadn't even got a DVD player, he'd think we were out of the Ark! The thing was Gus and I never spent many evenings in, with all the meetings we attended. He was asked to speak at so many Servicemen and Veterans conferences and jollies that followed, so when we did have an evening off, it was a luxury to sit by the fire just relaxing and mulling over the day.

That evening we did stay in and after supper, and I got my hymn book out.

"What hymns do you want for the wedding, Gus?" I asked, passing him the book. I moved my chair close up to his so that I could see which ones he was looking at.

"Clarice you know more about hymns than me. You've been going to the church a lot longer and didn't you say you used to sing in the choir?" he asked.

"Yes I did, but I want us to choose these together, it means a lot to me."

"Alright," he said "Find some hymns about everlasting love and I'll pick a couple." He grinned at me and his deep blue eyes sparkled.

I flicked through 'Pilgrimage' and 'Dedication' but it was hard to find 'Marriage' section. No wonder, because there were only three or four hymns listed, and I didn't know any of the tunes, or words come to that.

The 'Joy and thanksgiving' section, was more fruitful, though I suspected that the references made to love were more about loving God than each other. Finally we decided on 'The battle hymn of the republic' with its chorus of 'Glory,glory Hallelujah' That was a rousing tune and would certainly get everyone going, and the other one, we chose, with a tune well known to football supporters everywhere, was 'Love divine all loves excelling'. Gus was pleased with the choices.

"They'll raise the roof!" he said "Even I can sing those if I'm not too nervous"

"I don't want to walk down the aisle to the 'Wedding March' " I said suddenly,

"OK that's fine Clarice, but can I just ask why?"

I didn't want to tell him that the girls at school had often chanted the alternative words, as I walked in through the school gates, as a girl, they were

'Here comes the bride, big fat and wide' as most kids know. So I just told him I didn't like the tune, it was **so** hackneyed.

"That's OK then darling," he said "We'll ask the vicar to choose something else."

The next topic of conversation was the Honeymoon! Where to go?

I fancied somewhere remote and surrounded by sea, like the Scilly Isles or the rugged coast of North Devon, but as soon as I'd come out with it, I realised those sorts of terrain wouldn't be that suitable for Gus. I would have to let him chose. "What about Hawaii or if that's too far, what about Madeira?" he asked

He wanted sun and a five star hotel very near to the beach. He said he would rather swim in the sea, as he didn't think he'd be able to sunbathe or swim at the pool, as the kids might stare and some people might make comments.

I left Gus to decide the venue for our honeymoon. It could be my surprise!

Living our life together, I hadn't realised how restricted and vulnerable he felt. Now I was beginning to understand why he always wanted me with him; why we always mixed with Veterans, who understood and would view him as normal. In fact, more than normal, a hero! Otherwise we spent time with family or with the church people who were all totally accepting. The truth came home to me with a jolt. The limbs had healed, he could walk and drive; the night terrors and traumatic memories had been cured; but he could never feel whole, he could never feel normal. He was damaged goods. Oh how my heart bled for him!

There was much more for me to arrange.

I visited Irene at her Woodford salon.

"I! Guess what. I'm getting married again. She looked blank.

"What happened to the first one she said rather putting her foot in it. But it was my fault, I should have let her know about Terry's death. It was surprising that she hadn't read about it in 'the Sun', but maybe she hadn't realised he was my husband. I got her up to date with all my recent history, and she was both distressed at news of Terry's fatal accident, and happy that I'd 'bagged' a second husband, as she put it.

"Clarice, I'd love to set your hair . I can come over in the morning of the 14th and do it for you at home. I s'pose you still haven't learned to drive." I shook my head

"Never mind," Irene said, "I've got a new apprentice working for me now. She's very good at make-up. Would you like me to bring her over with me to do your face?" before I could answer she continued, "Course you'll have to pay her a bit of pocket money. Is that alright?"

"Yes, that's fine, what's her name?"

"Ginger" I made a face "Yes, well, her natural colour's ginger, but she dyes it blond. I think she was teased at school. That's how she got the name and it's stuck."

We nattered on about old times.

"By the way Clarice," she said changing the subject suddenly, "I saw that TV program with you on it. Why on earth didn't you tell us girls about it? We couldn't believe it was you! I say, you had some nerve walking down that cat walk with nothing on!"

"I did have something on. I had a body stocking on underneath those ribbons!"

I almost shouted, the mixture of shame and success coming back to me in a wave. I felt myself going scarlet.

"Calm down, you looked amazing" she said, patting my arm "The girls and I talked about it for days."

She went out to make a cup of tea, leaving me to recover my composure.

When I'd finished my tea, I told her she was welcome to stay for the wedding and reception and that Ginger could stay too if she liked. I gave her my address and telephone number and she said that they would arrive about two hours before the service.

On the bus home, I had a dreadful realisation! Four weeks to go and I hadn't booked caterers. I came out in a cold sweat. As soon as I got home, I rang round every caterer in the local directory and each said the same,

"I'm so sorry we're booked for June 14th. It is rather short notice." Yes, it was short notice and a complete oversight on my part. I had been so seriously considering little things little the choice of a hymn, when I should have been thinking about what the congregation were going to eat afterwards.

In desperation, and near to tears I rang Jo. I wondered how I, of all people, could have forgotten about the food? It must be love!

"Jo, guess what," I said, the second she picked up, "I've forgotten the caterers!"

"What do you mean you've forgotten them?"

"I mean 'they' don't exist. I haven't engaged any caterers. There isn't going to be anything to eat at the wedding, except my Mum's three tiered cake!"

There was a moment's silence, during which anyone but Jo would have cursed.

"Calm down Clarice", she said. "It's not the end of the world, I'm sure the ladies at the church can come up with something. They love that sort of thing. I'll find out and let you know. You'll have to pay though." She added as an afterthought. I knew money was always a bit of a sticking point with Jo as they only had Rod's income, and kids don't come cheap!

"Oh Jo, thanks a million!" she could not have known how grateful I felt.

"Lets meet for coffee tomorrow? My treat and we can talk it over."

"Yes OK. I'll ring round and investigate tonight and see you tomorrow. I'll have to bring the twins though."

"Then we'll go to Starbucks, they've got a big space at the back and I've seen mums and babies meeting up there. Can I borrow one of the boys and pretend he's mine?" She laughed

"Leave it with me and we'll go into the details tomorrow. Eleven, alright?"

We met the next day, for coffee, but no cakes for me! With four weeks to go I wanted to fit into that rather slim line dress.

Jo had phoned the Vicar's wife, Joan, first, out of courtesy, "I've been told her food isn't all that appetising. Don't say a word Clarice!" as she saw my laughter bubbling up,

"She may not be much of a cook, but she's very kind hearted." Added Jo, never wanting to say an unkind word about anyone.

"Anyway, Joan was happy about the idea and told me to phone Trish, the curate's wife who's done a cookery course at college."

"And did Trish say she would?" I asked biting my nails?"

"Yes" said Jo "She sounded quite excited, cooking for a war hero, and all that!... as well as your wedding, of course! She said she would get all the ladies together to discuss the menu, and who does what. But she thought a buffet would be easiest." Jo said the ladies at the church had cooked for so many garden parties, Harvest festivals and Fetes, that she was sure they would make a grand job of it. She said she thought they would do all the cooking and presentation free, but that I would have to give them money up front for the food and Gus would have to buy in the drinks. Booze was allowed in the Anglican Church buildings, but obviously could not be bought and sold. That meant we would have to pay for all the alcohol ourselves and not have a bar.

"Thank you soo much Jo. You wouldn't believe what a weight you've taken off my shoulders. I am just so relieved!" she smiled "And we only wanted a buffet. That's the beauty of a summer do, you don't need to sit down to a hot meal, and if you fancy soup you can have Gazpacho!"

"How many people will be staying after the Service . Have you any idea yet?" asked Jo.

"Well we haven't got a final head count, but we've had sixty acceptances, not counting family and close friends. It could go up to over a hundred." Jo's eyebrows shot up in alarm. Once again, if she hadn't been a Christian she might have sworn, instead, Jo managed a startled "Oh my goodness! Well, I suppose, if it's a fine day they can expand out into the church garden."

"Jo! Do you mean the Cemetery?"

"No, you idiot," it was her turn to giggle "We don't want them sitting on the grave stones eating their sausage rolls!"

"If we're going to let them loose in the garden we'll have to invest in plastic cups for the wine." I said, "We can't risk any accidents with smashed church glasses."

Dylan and Christie, yawned and turned towards each other in the double buggy. I thought they were going to wake up and cry, ending our chat, but Jo said they kept to a pattern, and would wake around one o' clock for their dinner. Jo said that having two was much easier than having just Meg, because the twins had each other.

"Shall I start the ball rolling then?" asked Jo

"Yes, please. As quick as you can, I've been frantic." I replied

"Stop worrying, Clarice, it's all in hand now. I've never known church suppers to be a let down, and the girls will try extra hard for you and Gus. Everyone's fond of you both."

"Before we go" added Jo "What's happening about the hens' and stags' nights?"

"Oh dear, I've been so carried away by the romance of it all I haven't given it a thought. I suppose Trevor will arrange something for the boys, it's not really my problem as long as Gus turns up at the church sober!"

"Rod won't mind baby-sitting. Why don't you and I leave all the rels and go out together, just the two of us?" asked Jo

"I'd absolutely love that." I said

"Right I'll fix it up and come and collect you. That's settled then. Where's Gus going to sleep the night before? He can't stay with you, It's bad luck."

"I thought you didn't believe in luck Jo" she laughed "OK then it's not the done thing!" She retorted. "I'll ask Rod if he minds Gus staying with us then. Then the two men can make their arrangements."

"Have you picked up Meg's dress yet?" I'd meant to check before. "The alterations must've been done by now." "Yes, I have" she said

"I'd love to see her in it."

"You will Clarice, on the day or come round before, if you like, for a preview."

"What will you be wearing Jo?" I asked

But she started to look hassled and put on her coat.

"Look we can talk to our hearts content on June 13th. Sorry but I have to run now, to get the boys back for their lunch. I'll ring you about all the arrangements and the costs as soon as. Must fly!"

And with that, she was gone.

It seemed a life time ago, that I had pushed Tom in his buggy!

Chapter 18

The great marriage machine rolled on.

Jo was as good as her word. The menu and pricing of the buffet food was agreed, and Trish and her ladies prepared and cooked and froze, ready for the big day. Though the catering was organised by Trish and the senior ladies of the church, Joan the vicar's wife was made to feel in ultimate control. Jo certainly knew her onions when it came to psychology!

The family arrived in the morning of June 13th. The men went to collect their hired suits and the women ironed and hung their dresses.

Mum took the cake round to the church rooms where, still in its separate tiers, it was locked up.

What had I forgotten? Probably something essential! I racked my brains.

Yes! The buttonholes! I phoned the florist straightaway and as soon as she heard my hysterical voice, she assured me that she could rustle up single carnations, including one for the long-suffering Rod, and they would arrive the next day with my bouquet.

All the family was settling in after their journey down from Cheshire and Gus had been driven off to into the night with the lads.

I heaved a huge sigh of relief when at last there was a knock on the front door. It was Jo, my rock, come to take me out for the evening. Hurrah!

She was all smiles as usual. Seeing her so happy and positive seemed to ease away all the tension of the day.

She had booked a table at a Bistro in Loughton, blue gingham cloths and paper serviettes.

We ordered a bottle of house red. I knew Jo did not drink and drive, ever, but tonight she would have just a drop, so that we could celebrate together, and then she would go on to water. I knew I could drink the rest of the wine myself, no problem. Why should I feel like this before what was to be the happiest day of my life? 'Yes,' I told myself 'This is a celebration, but I had had to do all the running, while Gus was working on his website and I am just wacked out. This must be why people employ a wedding planner, or, if they are young and very, very lucky, they get their mum to do it all for them.'

We ordered, and then made small talk about Meg's dress, how the colour suited her and what Jo was going to wear.

"My one and only posh dress." She said

As the drink soaked into my brain, I began to loosen up even more.

We chatted about the old days at the flat and at the Youth club, then the conversation inevitably turned to Rod whom she still adored.

"Jo," I started "I've got something to apologise to you about."

"What's that Clarice?"

"Well, I always kind of laughed about you and Rod keeping yourselves pure till you got married. I couldn't see the point. None of my family went to church or believed in God, so I was never taught about purity and that sort of thing." I blushed, not about talking of sex but at having to admit that I'd jeered at my best friend's standards.

"It's funny,"I said "Neither of us went to each other's first weddings." She looked hard at me, but before she could speak, I said "Oh, I'm so sorry. I put that very badly." She nodded,

"I mean I didn't come to your wedding and you didn't come to mine with Terry. It was a quick thing. We'd lost touch. I'm not sure you even had my address in Debden, did you?" I rushed on "I'm so glad it worked out well for you and Rod." She looked embarrassed.

"Look Clarice, it should be me apologising." She said "I never really said how sorry I was to hear about Terry being killed like that. It must have been terrible for you."

""Yes, I don't usually talk about it. It was the worst experience of my life. He was such a lovely, lovely man, and we were so happy, the three of us. It all started out as a bit of a gamble, the marriage I mean. I expect you guessed I was pregnant. Terry was the love of my life! Tom was devastated when he died, but he's done well. He's made a new life for himself up in Chester. When he left home," I continued, "I felt so alone. But Tom's only young, he needs to make a life for himself." Jo was drinking it all in, as I rattled on, the wine loosening my tongue. It was such a relief to get all this stuff off my chest. I could never have said a word to Gus, when he had so many burdens of his own to bear.

I shook myself out of the reverie. "But that's all in the past now and I need to focus on my future, which starts tomorrow, the next episode of my life!

The wine had taken effect and now I continued, almost oblivious of my listener.

"I was so lonely, and at a loss, then Gus came along and became the centre of my Universe! He needs so much help and support," I said, "and he's tremendously brave, as you know. But his false legs still cause him a lot of pain and trouble, from time to time. I won't go into the details, though," I added, in case Jo was as squeamish, "He is a true hero. He spends all his time helping other Army vets, you know. They all come back with problems and the Military is too short of cash to help them."

I felt a bit drunk and I wondered if I'd said too much.

I settled the bill on my card and we left the Bistro. Jo helped me into her car, and we drove off.

"Clarice," she said "has anyone ever told you that you're a hero too?"

I smiled at her. I was tipsy and I may have heard wrong.

Chapter 19

The 14th June found everyone at Violet cottage in a haze from the night before. I had left plenty of Chardonnay in the fridge and Port and lemon in the cupboard for Mum, her favourite.

We had the customary scrambled eggs and smoked salmon for a late breakfast washed down by pink champagne. I managed to force down half a piece of toast, while Mum stood over me.

"I don't want no scenes at the church with you fainting from lack of nourishment!" she told me. I could sense everyone was being extra nice, to me and to each other, to hide the usual wedding day nerves which pervade the bride's household, before the great event.

Flowers were delivered, hair was set, make-up applied, the tension rose.

At last, Mum and Prue helped me into my dress. It fitted perfectly! They said I looked beautiful, and Tom came up stairs and took his first photo!

By the time Tom said it was time to drive me to the church, everyone else had left to take up their pews. My heart was pounding, like a sledge hammer in my chest. I wished Jo was here to give me courage.

Tom could see I was in a state of nerves, so he cracked an awful joke,

"Hey Mum, he said you can relax, Gus might not turn up, we nearly got him legless in the pub last night." Despite myself, I giggled.

"Oh you are dreadful Tom! That's so tasteless. Lucky no one else, could hear you!"

"Mu-urm! It was only a joke to lighten you up a bit." He looked sheepish.

"No offence?" he said "None taken dearest," I answered, giving him a hug "It's only pre-wedding nerves." I said.

All that commitment and angst! All brides probably feel the same, I thought, it's only natural.' I thought to myself.

"Mum you **can** change your mind you know. It's been done before."

"No, thanks Tom, you are sweet. I'm just a bit stressed. You've no idea how much there's been to arrange. I just hope everyone has a good time."

"By the way Mum, you look terrific." Tom always knew how to boost me up. Then he added

"Dad would say you looked beautiful too. Maybe he's watching up there?"

My heart missed a beat. Not the time to think of Terry. The past is past.

'Look to the future, Clarice' I told myself firmly.

It was time to leave for the church. Tom had decided we must arrive seven minutes late. That was protocol! He helped me into the front seat of his ancient Ford. It wasn't posh, but he had cleaned it up for the occasion, and it was fairly roomy, in the front. Lucky I hadn't chosen a meringue though!

When we arrived at the church gate, Tom helped me out and handed me my bouquet. I thought how tall and handsome he looked in smart grey suit. A son to be proud of! I could see Jo was waiting with little Meg, looking like an angel in her satin dress.

"Now," He said as we walked up the path to the church door "when we get inside, Mum, I want you to take my arm and don't look to left or right as you walk down the aisle. I know you're nervous, but stay composed as if you were going to have your passport photo taken, okay?"

"Okay." I nodded, my mouth was very dry.

"And I will whisper when it's time to turn towards the altar." Tom said

"And don't look up at me either, alright?" he added

"Yes Tom," I said. I felt like a child; in that moment, our roles had been reversed.

Tom took me down the aisle to the strains of 'the Arrival of the Queen of Sheba'. I walked in time to the beautiful organ music, my head held high, I was imagining myself as the queen of Gus's heart. I could sense each row of the congregation turning to look at me as we processed towards the altar with Meg walking demurely behind.

Time stood still. I could see my darling Gus standing to the left of my brother.

Seeing him there waiting, my heart melted and all my pre-wedding fears dissolved away. We had come to love each other more and more deeply, since we first met, and this was our proclamation to the world!

A lot of water had flowed under the bridge, but he had hold on staunchly to our love even before I had committed to it. Coming to terms with his disabilities, had allowed me to fall hopelessly in love with this man. This hero, who had become my own personal hero, the centre of my universe!

As I reached him, I let go of Tom's arm and moved close to Gus. He squeezed my hand and smiled his wonderful smile.

Then David, the vicar, welcomed us together, as we stood in front of him.

He announced the first hymn, 'Love Divine all loves excelling'.

I tried to sing, but it's hard with a mouth dried by nerves!

As it ended, he asked us to kneel in front of him, while he prayed,

"Dearly Beloved, we are gathered together in the sight of God, and in the face of the congregation, to join together this man and this woman in Holy Matrimony"... it continued on and my mind wandered again. It ended with the words "... if any man can shew any just cause why they may not lawfully be joined together, let him now speak or else hereafter forever hold his peace."

There was a moment's silence and then a shrill voice called out from the back of the church "Yes, I can. I'm his wife!"

I felt footsteps walk over my grave.

I looked round. She was a thin woman in a mustard suit.

My head started to spin, my heart stopped and I felt the blood pool in my feet. All I remember was two men, my son and my brother, each grabbing an arm, and catching me before my head hit the marble.

It was true. Gus wrote to say that when he was nineteen he had married a girl, while he was stationed in Ireland. It hadn't lasted. He was posted abroad. He'd forgotten all about it? Could shell shock do that? Or did he realise that a Catholic girl wouldn't easily give him a divorce? Had he hoped it would all just go away: that she'd never catch up with him in England, it had been a long time ago?

He wrote again to ask forgiveness. 'Could we just go back to living together?'

He begged. He needed me. He relied on me.

But he had also lied to me.

The trust was gone. It was snuffed out in the 'twinkling of an eye'!

I didn't answer any of his letters.

Eventually he stopped begging, stopped writing.

Odessa's words came back to me. She had said 'there is a someone else in the shadows...he moves in and out of the distance in a strange way...its hard to define him.'

'She sure wasn't referring to Terry' I thought bitterly.

And so today, I shall regroup. It seems that all those years of consulting guides and sages, seers and therapists were wasted.

I was still the same old Clarice, hanging on to the edge by my finger tips.

Maybe Jo was right, 'Underneath are the everlasting arms.'

God is my only hope! Well...God, and of course Valium!